SUMMER 2009

Thank you John!

To my friend Nick, until we meet again.

TABLE OF CONTENTS

PREFACE

Would the twenty-year occupation of Afghanistan be considered a war? A conflict? A world peacekeeping mission? I suppose that depends on what you consider to be a war. The idea of war to most would be two nations engaging in an armed conflict over political or ideological differences. The majority of Americans imagine the clear-cut lines of World War 2 as a traditional war. One nation is attempting to conquer other nations, and as a result, armed conflict arises with distinctly different cultures and uniforms. The battles are all fought with a clear winner until one side concedes or is forced against their will to surrender. Afghanistan was not quite as black and white as that concept. It started with the idea of defeating an evil ideology that had declared war on the United States and everything that it stood for by committing the cowardly attacks on September 11th, 2001, but then became a military occupation focused on nation-building and installing a democracy into a country and culture that seemingly wanted no part of it.

In the midst of the varying political agendas surrounding Afghanistan, there was a generation of young men and women who were not only willing to be deployed there but in many cases more than excited to go. It was a chance to participate in history, to defend the ideals of America and the freedom it stands for on foreign soil against an evil ideology that wanted to hurt anyone and everyone who conflicted with their ways of life. In the aftermath of the 9/11 attacks, it was clear that the United States needed to take immediate action and seek justice and revenge. The problem was that there was no clear individual nation to declare war on. The enemy was an ideology that recruited fanatics into their ranks and could operate on a global scale. The focus of this threat was narrowed down to Afghanistan where the enemy seemed to have been operating freely.

The initial operations in Afghanistan were swift and decisive, with America firmly establishing that it was not going to lay down against an attack on its own soil. At the beginning, it all made sense. But as time went on, things got a little more complicated for some but not quite so complicated for a select group, the young men and women who were willing to be deployed there over and over as the conflict stretched on. To that group, it all made sense and it was as simple as going to Afghanistan in service of a country that they loved to protect the people they loved back home.

So much of war and history is lost in the bigger picture of what was occurring around the conflict or how it ended, but the real stories come from the personal experiences of the men and women who were there. The minds as young as 18 years old that were dealing with situations far beyond their understanding or even their ability to comprehend. Every single one of these volunteers has a story, a family, a past, and a future that may have been abruptly cut short because they believed so strongly in an idea that they decided was worth dying for.

JOINING THE MARINE CORPS

I joined the Marine Corps on June 19th, 2006, immediately after graduating high school. I don't believe that I had one exact reason for making that decision, but it was more a culmination of reasons. I knew I needed to get out of where I grew up. I didn't like the direction I saw my life going; I believed in service to the country, I needed a purpose greater than myself to guide me, and most of all, I wanted to make my mom and dad proud of me. The details of my boot camp experience are mostly inconsequential to telling this story. The only important detail is that I left for Parris Island with my high school friend Nick Xiarhos. We joined the delayed entry program together at 17 years old. It meant that we were committed to a four-year contract with the Marines, but because we weren't 18 yet, our parents had to sign for us and in the meantime we were held accountable by the local recruiter. At that time in my life, Nick was a friend who seemed to have it all figured out while most others around me were totally lost with some going in potentially very harmful directions in life. The year 2006 was when the opioid epidemic began to show its ugly face in the small community of Cape Cod and it was apparent that many high school kids were falling victim to it.

Nick and I were very different people in high school. We were part of the same friends group and knew each other well, but Nick was much more involved in the positive aspects of high school. He played sports, participated in extra school activities, and was loved by everyone. His leadership qualities and driven personality showed that he was destined for greatness. He gave off an aura of confidence, but never arrogant and was kind to everyone regardless of their social circle. I would describe myself as a very lost and confused kid in high school. My parents got divorced when I was 13 years old and I just never really recovered from it. I tried to fit in anywhere I could and that lack of identity made me feel like high school just wasn't for me. I played sports early on in high school, but after freshman year, I lost all interest in it and all interest in most aspects of high school. By my junior year, I began attending night school from 3-6 p.m. so that I could work during the day doing construction on concrete foundations to save money. Night school consisted mostly of troubled kids with very troubled home lives, and while that wasn't me, it caused me to start hanging around people that I probably shouldn't have been. It started becoming a real problem in my life and when I realized that I had no plan beyond high school, I started thinking that I wanted to join the military. One day, an Army recruiter randomly called my house and asked if I was interested in joining, so I said yes and set up a meeting with him and my mom at my mom's house. He came over and told me all about what the Army had to offer. I was very excited by everything he said and knew right then that the military was the path I wanted to go down. I set up another meeting with the recruiter at his office and went down there with the intent of getting more information to bring back to my mom so I could sign the paperwork and get things started.

When I walked into the recruiter's office, I saw that there were multiple offices for the different branches of the military. There were the Army, Navy, Air Force, and Marine Corps offices all in the same narrow hallway. As I walked up to the Army office, the Marine Corps recruiter came out of the office and asked what I was doing. I told him that I was there to talk with the Army recruiter and he looked at me and said, "How about you stop being a pussy and join the Marines?" As soon as he said that, I heard multiple people in his office start laughing and coming out to see who he was talking to. One of the people already in his office was Nick and I instantly started laughing when I saw him. At that moment, I decided to join the Marine Corps and told the Army recruiter that I was no longer interested. I wanted to be part of that aggressive and confident culture because I had never had that in my life. I was never the most confident person and was filled with self-doubt growing up. I knew that the Marines would be my chance to prove that I was more than I had always thought myself to be. Knowing that Nick was joining gave me the confidence to feel like we could get through it together. That was when we both signed up for the delayed entry program and had committed to a four-year enlistment contract.

We also signed up for what was called the "buddy program" where two recruits can sign up together and go to boot camp together and potentially stay in close proximity to each other for their entire enlistment. We both signed up to be infantry and wanted no part of any other job in the Marines. At the time, the wars in Iraq and Afghanistan were in full swing and we wanted to be part of both.

Nick and I held each other accountable for our commitment to join the Marines.

We weren't just telling everyone we planned on doing it, we were already signed up and we made sure we both reminded each other of that whenever we started doing stupid 17-year-old kid things. It made me completely change my mindset and life as it became my only focus. We also made it a point to leave as soon as possible after graduating high school so that we wouldn't have the entire summer to party with friends and lose focus. We started as casual friends but became best friends through our commitment to the Marines. I looked up to Nick in many ways as a role model during that time. I didn't want to let him down and I felt that the fact we were going to boot camp together meant that I had a commitment to him, too. During the delayed entry program, we did physical training with the recruiter twice a week and ran for miles. We also did a field trip to New Hampshire to do a mock boot camp with other kids in the delayed entry program from all over Massachusetts. It was not what I'd call a fun time, but it made us both feel even more committed to the Marines. Joining the Marines became our identity in many ways. It was all talked about, all we thought about, and all we looked forward to. We had some slightly older friends that were already in the Marines and we asked them nonstop questions about what to expect. As the time to leave got closer, the reality started to sink in that we were leaving our hometowns for the first time in our lives to become part of something much bigger than ourselves. I was nervous and still had a lot of self-doubt, but I knew that if Nick was going with me I would be fine. He had a way of making everything seem so much simpler and manageable than I felt they were in my constantly overthinking mind.

We arrived at the Marine Corps Recruit Training Depot Parris Island in late June but were separated during the first week due to a bee allergy that was discovered in Nick's medical file, which caused him to be put into a holding platoon while I continued forward with training. This was devastating as we had planned on going through boot camp together and hopefully onto further training together. For all, Nick knew at the time he was going to be medically discharged from the Marines and he was beside himself. When you first arrive at the boot camp, you are placed into an intake platoon with all the other newly arrived recruits in order to complete administrative tasks before getting placed into your official training platoon. The platoon had its own separate squad bays with bunk beds, so Nick and I grabbed one to bunk together. I remember being in the squad bay one morning and a drill instructor came through the door and in a booming voice, yelled out, "Xiarhos!" Nick ran over to the drill instructor, stood at attention, and was then told to report to the medical building. I had no idea why this was happening and saw Nick run out of the squad bay. I continued with the intake process during the day and when I returned to the squad bay later that afternoon, I saw Nick packing his bag in an agitated manner. He then told me that our recruiter messed up his medical file and didn't include in it that he was allergic to bees, which Nick had disclosed early on in the enlistment process. He then told me that he was getting sent to a medical holding platoon and had no idea what was going to happen to him. He was so upset at the time that he was fighting back tears, but also angry at the recruiter for causing the issue. I felt scared and alone in that moment, knowing that Nick was leaving and I most likely wouldn't see him for the rest of boot camp. Everything up until that point we had done together and now we'd both be on our own while potentially being sent in different directions, which could affect our entire enlistment going forward. I knew that I had the ability to get through boot camp on my own, but it was an experience we had planned on sharing together since we first made the decision to join the Marines. Nick ultimately ended up being delayed for about two weeks and continued with no further issues, but was sent to a different training company in a totally different area of Parris Island. I remember seeing him only one time during that period and it was when both of our training companies were at the rifle range in late July. I randomly saw him in a chow hall line for the first time since we got separated in late June. At the time, I could see that he was a squad leader, which wasn't the least bit surprising to me as Nick always took the lead in everything he did in his life. You are not allowed to speak out or turn to other recruits during boot camp, but seeing each other was a great feeling and a huge relief to me to know that he had continued with training. We looked at each other and smiled, laughing inside at how crazy and intense the boot camp experience was. It was like we were both thinking to ourselves in a comical way, "What the hell are we doing here?"

I was not a standout recruit in any way whatsoever. In fact I tried to blend in and draw no attention to myself. I was never a good athlete in school and was never the most confident or outgoing person either. I simply wanted to make it through training with no major setbacks.

Unfortunately, about halfway through boot camp, I started feeling a throbbing pain in my groin area. I assumed it was some sort of pulled muscle so I ignored it in fear that if I were to report it, I would get dropped from my platoon and not graduate on time. As time went on it got worse and I developed a serious limp when I walked and ran. As the training intensified and we did more hiking with packs and running in boots, the pain got to a point where it was nearly unmanageable. My desire to graduate on time and not be medically dropped was my biggest motivation to keep going. I began to favor the uninjured side when I walked and ran, which caused that side to develop a great deal of pain as well. I remember being within one week of graduation and doing a formation run in boots when I felt a pop in my right hip that instantly crippled me with pain. I tried to keep up but was limping so badly that all I could do was fall out of the run and off to the side. After that, it became clear to my drill instructors that I needed to get medical attention and I was sent to the aide station. The doctors did an x-ray on my hips and saw that both had serious stress fractures going through the ball joints that connect the leg bones to the pelvic bone.

When they told me that I needed immediate surgery, I lost all composure. I cried and begged them to let me go back to my platoon to graduate with them as it was only days away. It was the most devastating news I could have possibly received. I knew that the injury was bad, but I honestly thought that if I just made it through graduation I'd be able to go home on leave and deal with the issue then.

At that point it was so close to my graduation date that my mom, younger sister Lynsey, older brother Jon, and grandmother were already on their way down to South Carolina to see me graduate. They were on their flight when a Marine from Parris Island made a phone call to my mom to inform her that I was going in for surgery, but because she was already on the flight, the call went to her voicemail. When they all landed and got off the plane, my mom turned her cell phone on and listened to the voicemail. The message did not say what the surgery was for, but only that I was having a procedure done that would prevent me from graduating while also giving them the location of the hospital where it was being done. My family went from the joy and excitement of anxiously waiting to see my graduation from Marine Corps boot camp to the disturbing news that I was in a hospital somewhere in South Carolina having an unknown surgery.

I had surgery that same day and woke up in a hospital bed the next morning with my mom in the room, who I hadn't seen in three months. My brother, sister, and grandmother came in shortly after but my mom sitting in the corner on a chair was the first thing I saw. I was so sad that I could barely feel any excitement in seeing her, and I thought that I had failed at the one thing I wanted more than anything in my life. At that point I had already completed all of the required training of boot camp, so I technically still graduated but without the ceremony of walking across the famous Parris Island parade deck and receiving the coveted Marine Corps Eagle Globe and Anchor. At that point, it was the most important thing in the entire world to me, and I was devastated to miss out on it. My drill instructors knew how difficult this must have been for me to endure that injury for so long and have my body give out at the very end, so they did their own ceremony for me in the hospital room with my mom, brother, and sister, and grandmother there. It was an extremely powerful gesture done by them that will stick with me for the rest of my life. Once

Nick graduated, he also came to see me in the hospital with his family and we caught up for the first time since getting separated in June. It was great to see him but depressing for me to know that he'd be going on to infantry school while I remained in the hospital. Our plan to stick together in the Marines was once again ruined. I had no idea where Nick would end up in the coming months and at the time, I thought there was a high likelihood that I'd be medically discharged for my injuries. I had no idea what my future held and felt like my life was over, that I would be discharged and my dream ruined.

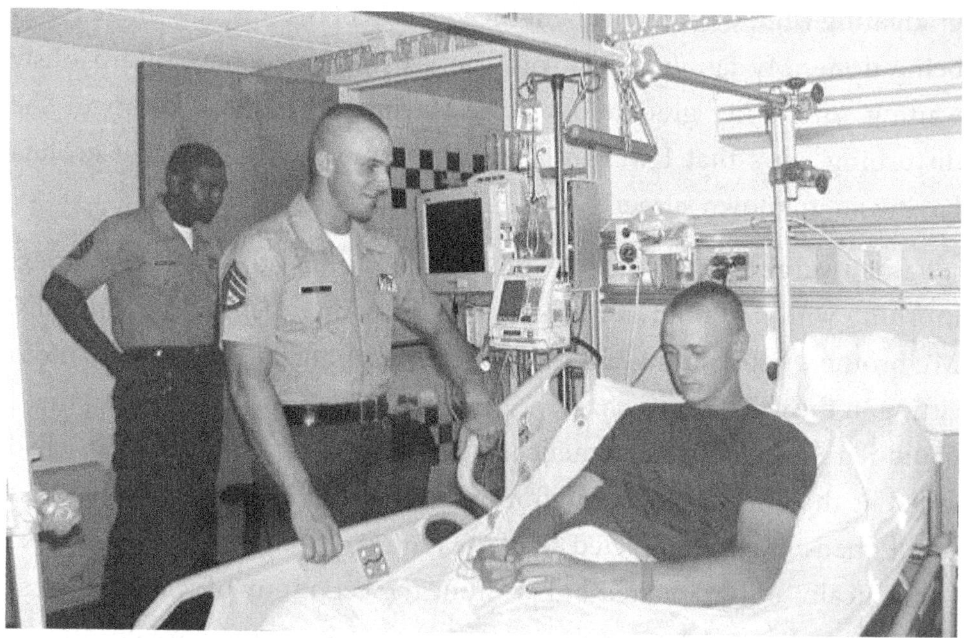

My Senior Drill Instructor presenting me with the Eagle Globe and Anchor.

After my surgery, I stayed in the Naval Hospital in South Carolina for two months doing rehabilitation and physical therapy. It was a strange time because I was mostly left entirely by myself but still in the intense environment of Parris Island. It was a very lonely time for me, but it was my first real lesson on how to accept a bad situation and move on from it. After I left the hospital, I was sent back to Parris Island to what was called a Basic Marine Platoon. It was for recruits who had graduated from Boot Camp but were too injured to go on to further training. I arrived there and it became immediately obvious to me that the majority of the people there were just trying to get a medical discharge from the Marine Corps and had no intention of moving forward past their seemingly minor injuries compared to mine. There was a comically fat guy there who had been in the platoon for so long that he attained the rank of Lance Corporal, which normally takes 18 months to be promoted to. He was insufferable to be around and felt that he deserved some kind of respect from the other Marines there, but he was so fat that he couldn't even do the physical training with us. To this I think about that kid and it still makes me a little angry. I would say that my time in that Basic Marine Platoon was the worst part of my entire enlistment. I felt I was in limbo while Nick had moved forward to the fleet and I was surrounded by mostly weak people with horrible victim mentalities. I was also concerned that because of my injuries, I would have to switch out my infantry MOS (Military Occupational Specialty) into something non-infantry. This was something I simply would not allow. I joined the Marines to be in the infantry during wartime. Nick was also infantry and at that point he was already at the School of Infantry in North Carolina. I rehabbed my injuries like my life depended on it. I walked every day until I could run, and then I ran every day until I could complete the required three miles in under 28 minutes to move on from the platoon. I was in that Basic Marine Platoon for a month and a half before leaving for the School of Infantry.

When someone joins the Marine Corps and gets a contract for infantry, it is basically an open contract. Your specific job within the infantry is not decided until you get to the School of Infantry where you are given a wishlist of jobs and then placed where you are most needed. Due to my double broken hip injury, I felt that being a basic rifleman that hikes with heavy gear on my back nonstop would almost certainly cause me to break them again that early after my recovery. I learned that the MOS of 0352 (anti-tank missile-man) involved being primarily vehicle mounted and would be much safer to allow my injuries to continue to recover. I wanted to be a basic rifleman more than anything, but I also knew that it could very likely result in injuring myself again and cause me to get medically discharged from the Marines. By the time I began Infantry School Nick had already made it to the fleet Marine Corps and was assigned to 1st Battalion 9th Marines on Camp Lejeune, North Carolina, a short drive from the School of Infantry. I spoke with him as often as I could to get insight into what to expect during infantry training and get any advantage I could. I managed to graduate from Infantry school with no issues and was assigned to 2nd Light Armored Reconnaissance Battalion (LAR), also on Camp Lejeune and a short distance from Nick's battalion.

I quickly learned the ways of the fleet Marine Corps and settled into my living situation. In the spring of 2008, Nick and I were both scheduled to deploy to Iraq but to different areas. My battalion did the seven months of training to prepare to deploy, then left for Iraq in April 2008.

By that time, the war in Iraq had been mostly stabilized and there was not nearly as much kinetic combat as the previous five years. It was still a dangerous place, it just greatly depended on where you were and when you were there. I was in a quick reaction force platoon as a light supporting machine gunner but saw no real combat the entire seven months. We dealt with some IEDs (Improvised Explosive Devices) that we discovered, but we were able to do controlled detonations to them before they injured anyone. The deployment was uneventful and I returned in October 2008 with some experience and the ability to tell the new guys that I had deployed to Iraq while they hadn't, which was a huge deal at the time.

When you get to the fleet Marine Corps, there are those who have deployed and those who haven't. Once you deploy, you fall into a category of no longer being considered a new guy and your life drastically improves. Having that deployment under my belt was a good feeling and the experiences gained from it made me feel ready for another one. I knew the deployment wasn't what I had hoped for and felt like I hadn't accomplished what I was looking to prove within myself. It hardly dawned on me how lucky we all were to deploy with our entire battalion and come home with everyone. My idea of war was distorted by the desire to prove myself in combat and be part of history.

Nick's time in Iraq was spent in the infamous city of Ramadi where a massive battle to take control of the city had occurred in 2006. The city was considered somewhat stable by 2008 but it was still a dangerous place. On April 22, 2008, a suicide bomber in a large truck filled with 2,000 pounds of explosives drove full speed toward the entrance to Nick's combat outpost. Two Marines on guard duty, 19-year-old Jordan Hearter and 21-year-old Jonathan Yale, saw the truck coming and made the courageous choice to stand their ground and open fire on the truck with machine guns. The truck proceeded toward the gate but with the driver dead from the Marines gunfire, it slowed down without making it through the gate and into the base filled with 150 Marines and Iraqi police. The truck exploded and killed Jordan and Jonathan while leveling a whole city block. I had heard about this when I was in Iraq but did not realize the severity of it or how closely Nick was involved in the incident.

During that time in Iraq, the United States had been there for so long that many of the bases were set up with computer centers and internet. Both mine and Nick's bases had small ones and we would communicate through Facebook once in a while. I got promoted to the rank of Corporal during my Iraq deployment and messaged Nick to tell him. He responded by telling me about the suicide bomber but did not give any details other than he was fine. At the time, I had no idea how serious the whole event was.

Nick and I returned at the same time and our families rented condos in Topsail Island, North Carolina, right outside of Camp Lejeune. We partied and had a great time while we celebrated our deployment and coming home safely from it. I never had any real conversation with Nick about that suicide bomber because that wasn't how young Marines did things. Marines didn't sit around and talk about traumatic experiences in a vulnerable way, we just drank and had fun while pretending that we were completely unfazed by anything and everything. I had no idea at the time but I'm sure that Nick's outlook on life drastically changed after experiencing that traumatic event. He never showed any change to me and was the same Nick I always knew and we continued right where we left off before we went to Iraq.

We spent our weekends partying in Wilmington, North Carolina and Myrtle Beach, South Carolina as often as we could. At that time we were both 21 years old and reckless as could be. It was some of the most fun times of my life. We began making friends with those who attended the University of North Carolina Wilmington and started partying there like we were just any other college kids.

We'd train during the week with our units on Camp Lejeune then meet up on Friday to hop in Nick's jeep and head out of the back gate of Camp Lejeune to make the 45-minute rides to Wilmington. We'd stop at the liquor store on the way down to stock up on booze then get to our friends' apartment and start partying without a care in the world. While we were owned by the Marine Corps most of the time, we felt that we could be whoever we wanted in Wilmington. We felt that we were living the best days of our lives and the grind of being in the infantry and wearing ourselves out all week made the experiences even better. On Sundays we'd limp out of town hungover and try our best to mentally prepare for what we knew would be a rough Monday morning.

Nick and I partying at UNCW with our friends Max and Matt.

PREPARING FOR AFGHANISTAN

The standard deployment rotation for a Marine Battalion back then was seven months of deployment followed by 14 months back in the United States. I spent most of my post-deployment leave back home in Cape Cod, Massachusetts and it consisted of drinking heavily with my friends while visiting them at the colleges they were attending. After I returned to Camp Lejeune I settled back into the fleet Marine Corps lifestyle and began to wonder when the next deployment would be. Several months went by and rumors started circulating about Afghanistan and a major troop surge that was being planned by President Obama. The Taliban had essentially taken back the entire southern area of Afghanistan called the Helmand Province and were freely running their opium trade that funded the majority of their operations. The war in Iraq had been the primary focus of the Marine Corps since 2003, so the majority of deployments were sent there. The United States had been in Afghanistan since 2001 but it didn't seem to me that it was discussed anywhere near as much as Iraq. In the summer of 2008, my battalion had sent a platoon to support 1st Battalion 6th Marines on a deployment to the Helmand Province.

Many of the Marines who went were close friends of mine and they came back with stories drastically different from my experiences in Iraq. They described it as the Wild West, the Taliban running freely and openly engaging U.S. forces with bold attacks. It sounded like everything I was hoping for.

I cannot recall exactly when the official news came about, but the entire battalion was informed that company C (Charlie) would be deploying to Afghanistan in May of 2009 as part of a Marine Expeditionary Brigade. A Marine Expeditionary Brigade, or MEB, is a Marine air- ground task force that consists of approximately 10,000 Marines and sailors constructed to support a reinforced infantry regiment. The Brigade is assigned a specific mission and all of the various elements attached to the brigade have a specific mission of their own within the bigger picture. Our specific mission and role involved in taking back control of a portion of the Helmand Province from the Taliban did not allow for an entire Light Armored Reconnaissance battalion but only a company of approximately 150 Marines and sailors supported by a headquarters and support element. The entire battalion would have been ideal for this mission but for reasons far above my level of understanding, it was decided that an enhanced company would suffice with the potential for another company to follow later in the operation. For this reason, 2nd LAR battalion selected Charlie Company to deploy but rearranged the entire company by handpicking Marines that they felt were best suited for the deployment. I was selected to go to the weapons platoon of Charlie Company as a gunner for an anti-tank variant of an LAV (Light Armored Vehicle)-25.

Light Armored Reconnaissance Battalions consist of four line companies supported by a headquarters and support company that all employ LAV-25s in platoon-sized elements of four vehicles. The LAV-25 is essentially a small tank with wheels and a 25-millimeter cannon on top, with a rifle squad in the rear that is deployed as infantry. They are extremely versatile and fast compared to tanks while packing serious firepower with the cannon on top. They are ideal for desert warfare and rapid advances across enemy-occupied territory. Every company also has a weapons platoon that consists of mortars and anti-tank weapons. The weapons platoon is distributed throughout the four platoons as support.

My specialty in anti-tank and armor is what caused me to be selected. The anti-tank variant of the LAV-25 has a turret mounted on the top that fires two TOW (Tube launched Optically tracked Wire guided) missiles that are designed to destroy tanks, armor, buildings and anything else that gets in the way of the Marines on the ground. It is basically a large missile that is launched it of a tube with a wire on the back of it that is attached to the turret. The wire directly connects to the sights that the gunner uses to guide the missile as it moves toward its target.

LAV-AT (Anti-tank Variant)

LAV-25

Once the newly formed and hand-picked Charlie Company was selected, the training for Afghanistan began. A pre-deployment work up usually consists of a standard and precisely scheduled series of training exercises that culminate in a final evaluation that determines if the battalion is considered to be battle and deployment ready. In our case, the deployment to Afghanistan was so rushed and had so many other elements involved that we were unable to attend the usual training exercises and had to outsource the Army's bases for several of them. This created an expedited training cycle, but I felt it was far more effective because everyone knew that the mission was going to be dangerous and fast-paced. There was a sense of urgency that drove everyone and brought out the best in us. Everyone was excited and you could feel it in the air. One thing you have to understand about the Marine Corps infantry is that they WANT to be in combat. They WANT to be sent to the worst part of the worst battlefield to test what they have trained for so long to do. It is a point of pride amongst the infantry and the mindset of young Marines that are eager to test themselves on the battlefield. It is what young men join the Marines for, and what they dream to do. This applied to me just as much as anyone else. I wanted to go to combat and I wanted to kill the enemy. I wanted the adrenaline rush and pride of knowing that I defended my country in the purest form possible. I felt that my deployment to Iraq was a major letdown and I wanted to prove myself by doing what I had joined the Marines to do. This way of thinking is vital to the entire United States Military. I can only speak on the Marine Corps because that is my only experience, but I have no doubt that all other services have the same feelings.

There is no greater example of this way of thinking than my friend Nick Xiarhos. Once Nick learned that I was deploying to Afghanistan, he immediately began to figure out a way to go too. He had been around my friends who went there in 2008 and heard all the same stories I had. He wanted a part of the action and couldn't sit back while I went. He had heard that 2nd Battalion 8th Marines was deploying and had met many Marines from that unit when his battalion relieved them in Ramadi, Iraq the previous year. Nick had formed a close relationship with a lieutenant platoon commander and reached out to him to see if he could initiate him being transferred from his current battalion to 2/8. It didn't take long for the transfer to go through and Nick was slated to deploy to Afghanistan as part of the same Marine Expeditionary Brigade as me. Nick completely volunteered for a deployment that he did not have to go on. He wanted to be part of history and knew that the mission was as dangerous as it came. This was different from Iraq in 2008. We knew that the Taliban had taken control of this territory and our sole mission was to take it back. We knew that there would be enemy contact and we were excited as hell for it.

There is another critical aspect of this mindset that I did not fully realize until years later and feel I must mention. I have a difficult time putting into words the amount of respect I have for the Marines and Sailors with wives and children who deployed. It is one thing to go into a combat zone for seven months as a young man who has no real responsibility beyond themselves, but it is an entirely different thing to do it when there are people who you love and are depending on you back home. The same can be said for the older Marines and Sailors who had been around long enough to have seen the beauty of the world and knew full well what they were missing out on. I felt that I was so naive to most of life at the time that nothing mattered but what was right in front of me. I cannot imagine the person I am now in many of these situations because I am too enlightened about how beautiful life is and the world we live in. That is not to say I wouldn't serve this country again in a time of need if I had the chance to, but I would have a drastically different outlook on the seriousness of the situation and what was at stake. The cause would need to be justified beyond all doubt.

This brings me to where I feel this story really starts. This is not a war story or an account of a military operation in great detail. This is the story about my thoughts as a 21-year-old young man. I'd call myself more of a child at that time, and how I processed my deployment to Afghanistan and everything that occurred. I kept a journal in Afghanistan, and not the type of journal you use as an adult to plan your life and career, and release your feelings. This was a notebook a friend gave me and I simply decided to start writing down how I was feeling while detailing what was occurring around me. I recently found this notebook in my basement amongst other old Marine Corps memories and began reading it. I wrote these journal entries at 21 years old and I am now 36. This story will be told through these journal entries and will be unedited except for names that I feel need not be included that are irrelevant to the story. It will be obvious what the journal entries are by the terrible grammar and the italics they are written in. I will also add comments to explain certain things that may not make sense to the reader. Some entries are nothing more than me complaining about a miserable situation, and some are life-altering moments. There is a story within these journal entries that transcends the seventh months I spent in Afghanistan and the tiny role I played in a massive military campaign called Operation Khanjar, an Arabic word meaning strike of the sword. So much of my life revolves around that short time period and I feel that writing this is the therapeutic release that I've needed for the last 15 years. This story is told through my eyes and memories of what occurred on that deployment. It is not an account of the entire operation but only the small role that I played in it and how it affected me.

STEPPING OFF

May 8, 2009

Still in Kyrgyzstan (a stopping point to enter Afghanistan) and my sleep schedule is still messed up so I woke up at four am and went to breakfast with Markusic (my closest friend in my platoon). We came back and SSGT Hayes (my platoon sergeant who I greatly respected) was pissed about something so now we have to go everywhere in groups of four. I went to the gym to take my mind off things for a while, came back to shower and went to lunch. Some people in this platoon are really starting to piss me off already which is a bad sign. I hear we are leaving tonight to go to Afghanistan which is a good and bad thing I guess. Everything is still unorganized and no one knows what's going on. I don't even think that we're going to start operating for a month. I feel very alone out here sometimes and it seems like everyone has a girl back home but me. I wish I stilled talked to (girl I was briefly talking to before I left) but I guess she doesn't want to so I'm not even going to bother. It would just be nice to have someone to talk to through all of this.

May 9, 2009

Who cares? I got to keep telling myself that every time I start to get miserable about this shit. We got to Afghanistan today and it looks just like Iraq except less set up. They got us living in these big white tents with no AC and it's hot as hell. That's the only real problem I got with this place.

I keep having really weird mood swings lately. I'll feel excited about everything one minute and then just feel really depressed the next, it's starting to get to me I guess. A lot of it has to do with back home and back in North Carolina. I feel like I was really starting to make some good friends down there in UNCW(University of North Carolina Wilmington) and when I get back they'll all be gone. I'm also sort of scared of getting back and getting out because I don't really know what I'm going to do. I feel like this is the last big obstacle I have and then everything is going to start working for me and I'll be happy with my life. I hope this deployment is everything it's been built up to be so it goes by fast.

May 10, 2009

Today I woke up at 0530 and went to the gym to avoid any stupid things that could be going on in the tent. I went to breakfast and then to the phone center to call my mom to let her know what's going on. Gozno (Gabriel Gonzales, my vehicle commander at the time) thinks he has cancer on his nuts and I really hope he doesn't because he would have to go home. I hung out in the little movie theatre until lunch then came back to the tent and saw that they put floors in which is awesome. I still can't believe that I'm actually on a deployment again. I'm starting to think less and less about back home because like I said before, who cares? I really just want to start operating to get things moving and to see what happens. No one has really pissed me off today which I am pretty happy about.

Gabriel Gonzales ended up being sent back to the United States for his medical issues and I became the vehicle commander in his place. I was sad to see him go but happy to take his place as vehicle commander. The change moved my friend Chad Williams to my vehicle gunner, who proved to be my right-hand man on that deployment. He was one of the most resourceful and quick-thinking people I'd ever met.

May 11, 2009

Today was basically the same as yesterday except we had to do some really stupid classes on weapons systems that we already fully know just to kill time really. It felt so much hotter out today than it has been lately. I can't stand it, I sweat from the time I wake up until the time I go to sleep. We also got a briefing this morning on the area that we are in and it is actually much worse than I thought it was as far as the number of Taliban. When things kick off it should get pretty interesting. I went to the phone center and got on the computer at lunch. I didn't have any new messages. I did send (a friend from back home) a message on Myspace though. Her mom died recently and I feel really bad for her. It seems like a sandstorm rolls through this place every day and it's really fucking annoying. Nick (Xiarhos) should be here with 2/8 (2nd Battalion 8th Marines) soon. Hopefully I'll see him and I can laugh at him for volunteering to come to this miserable place. I miss everyone but I try to put in the back of my head to keep from going crazy out here.

May 21, 2009

Things feel like they are starting to happen now. The command knows when were are pushing out and what our mission is but they won't tell us because of OPSEC (operational security). The company also has all of its vehicles now including our four AT's (anti-tank variant of LAV-25) which I'm pretty excited about. We are still doing classes every day but it's a lot better than some stuff that we could be doing. I'm still waiting on Nick to get here, his battalion lives in the tent right behind us. I should be able to see him all the time because we are operating with them.

These journal entries were an account of the long and convoluted journey that it took to get from the United States to Afghanistan and the confusion that came along with a deployment so hastily thrown together.

The Marine Corps has a way of keeping you constantly uncomfortable, which results in a lot of bitching amongst Marines. It is part of the culture and the way it will always be. If Marines aren't complaining or unhappy, then something is seriously wrong. This deployment was unique because we had only deployed with one company of approximately 150 Marines and Sailors with a headquarters and support element. Typically an entire battalion of approximately 1000 Marines and Sailors would deploy. Because we were such a small element, we felt very close-knit from the Battalion Commander, Lt. Col. Grattan, a fellow Massachusetts native who would always talk about the Boston Red Sox to anyone of any rank, down to the lowest ranking Marine. It was a unique situation that only added to the feeling that this deployment was something different.

The process of getting to Afghanistan is quite unpleasant. Everyone flies in commercial airliners with all of their gear for hours on end until they reach Germany. From Germany, you take a commercial flight again into Kyrgyzstan, and then from Kyrgyzstan you fly in a military aircraft to Kandahar Air Base in Afghanistan. From Kandahar you fly in large helicopters to whichever forward operating base you happen to be assembling at. In our case, this was an outpost called Camp Leatherneck that had been specifically built up for the purpose of assembling the Marine Expeditionary Brigade that we were a part of to invade Helmand Province in Southern Afghanistan. During the transit you are never comfortable. You are either extremely bored or busy going through various gear and recording the serial numbers over and over. When that is done, there is usually some other meaningless task that is thought of in order to keep the Marines busy so they don't get too complacent or into some sort of trouble. Bored and complacent Marines will come up with ridiculous activities to occupy themselves and many times, they result in them getting injured or in some kind of trouble. It is comical, but in hindsight, I can see why the leadership needed to constantly come up with tasks to be done. To try and control young men and the toxic masculinity that comes with the environment is a difficult thing to do and the best way to do it is by keeping them so busy and pissed off that they have no time to do anything else. This concept is what drives the Marine Corps infantry and keeps it aggressive and angry. Both are strongly needed.

After the journal entry on May 21st, Nick did arrive in Afghanistan but I cannot recall the exact date. I remember the first time I saw him there as clear in my mind as though it happened yesterday. I was sitting in the hot tent on my cot listening to my iPod when I heard someone call out my name. In the military, everyone goes by their last names so I heard "COVILLE!" Yelled from across the tent. I then saw Nick walking in and he looked at me and said, "Well if it isn't the gayest man in the Marine Corps!" I can't remember our exact conversation after that but we talked about the upcoming operation and where we were going to be relative to one another. We learned that Nick was going to a city called Garmsir and I was going to a city called Khan Neshin in the southernmost area of the Helmand Province, right near the border of Pakistan. We would be approximately 50 kilometers apart so it was considered the same area of operations. We then went outside and met up with another friend of ours who was in 2/8 named Jon Quiceno, or Q as we called him. Q had also volunteered to go on the deployment with Nick and was transferred in the same manner from 1st Battalion 9th Marines. When we were back home, Nick, Q, and I partied together every weekend in Wilmington, North Carolina. I met Q through Nick and he became a close friend of mine. We all caught up and took pictures together with the small digital cameras we had brought along. I saw Nick and Q a few more times at Camp Leatherneck before we parted ways for our separate missions but the training and preparation started to intensify, so the meetings were fewer and shorter. It was such a strange thing for two kids from Cape Cod, Massachusetts to be sitting together in southern Afghanistan while joking and smoking cigarettes like it was just any other day. I felt like our original plan to join the Marines together had come full circle. We were exactly where we were supposed to be and everything from the beginning when we first enlisted together in that delayed entry program had led us to that moment.

We continued our training at Camp Leatherneck and made the final preparations for our gear and vehicles to push south. We learned that we were leaving ahead of the rest of the main body of the invasion force because of our versatile LAV-25s and the fact that we were traveling the farthest south. The rest of the infantry elements were to be inserted during the night by helicopter in their various areas of operations. All of us knew that we were going into enemy territory. There was no question that we would see combat and strangely I was not afraid, only excited and nervous. I felt like I was lucky to be there.

Nick and I at Camp Leatherneck

OPERATION KHANJAR BEGINS

On June 28, we pushed off for Khan Neshin. We left in our enhanced company-sized convoy and traveled south into completely unknown enemy territory. Camp Leatherneck was its own small city in the middle of the desert in Helmand Province. It was surrounded by desert as far as the eye could see and once you left the gates, it was like going into an open ocean of sand with huge mountains in the distance that never seemed to get any closer. All of our movements were done at night with blackout conditions; this means we had no lights on and only used night vision goggles while the drivers had enhanced night vision screens. This was a stressful thing because in Afghanistan at night, there is no light pollution. This means that if it is a full moon, it is nearly as bright as day and if there is no moon, it is so dark that you can't even see your hand in front of your face. There was no moon when we started our journey so it was very dark and disorienting. We followed the vehicle in front of us and kept in radio contact with updates on when and where to stop. Many vehicles got stuck in the loose desert sands and had to be pulled out, delaying the entire convoy. It was a huge and stressful mess trying to get the vehicles unstuck in total darkness. I could tell over the radio that our battalion commander, Lt. Col. Grattan was starting to get annoyed by the delays but there was nothing we could do about it. It was like driving through sand dunes on a beach at certain points and there was no way to tell when that loose sand would appear with the night vision goggles on.

We would assemble during the day in a company-sized circle of security with our vehicle guns facing outward and took turns sleeping. The only place to sleep was either on top of the vehicles, inside the vehicles, or on the ground. Luckily for my crew and I, we had decided to steal four cots from Camp Leatherneck as we anticipated this exact situation. The cots folded up and didn't take up too much space, so we felt taking them was of the utmost importance. We were all thankful for those cots and used them whenever possible, but there were many times when setting up a cot wasn't an option and we slept in the vehicle or on the ground. The trip down was exciting because we knew that we were going into unknown territory where we would be operating on our own and figuring it out as we went. With each day of travel that passed, we could see more signs of civilization as the open desert became greener as we got closer to the Helmand River.

Charlie Co. staged and ready to make the journey south.

We left Camp Leatherneck on June 28 and arrived in Khan Neshin on July 2nd. July 2nd was the official start date of operation Khanjar for the entire Marine Expeditionary Brigade. We set up our vehicles on the outskirts of the main town area and waited for the sun to come up.

When daytime arrived, we saw local Afghan people going about their business with extremely confused and suspicious looks on their faces. Most of them looked like they lived in peasant times from hundreds of years ago. The men had long beards and it was hard to tell their age because they looked so rough from living in those primitive conditions. That particular region of Afghanistan had not been occupied by foreigners since the Russians in the 1980's so I'm sure it was a surprise for them to see us appear out of nowhere. I thought about how many of the older men had probably fought against those Russian forces and were no strangers to war and foreign invaders trying to take their lands. I also had the thought that maybe they expected us and had been waiting for that very moment. There was an eerie feeling of quiet in the air that we could all sense but kept to ourselves. The rifle squads dismounted the back of the LAV-25s and began searching through the town and trying to establish an area of operation and command posts. The town consisted of compacted houses made of mud with six-foot-high walls around many of them that served as property marking barriers. Some were spread far apart and others were so close to each other that they formed their own small compounds. The area was much greener with vegetation than I'd imagined it would be because of the Helmand River running through the middle of the region. There were also big irrigation canals that ran through the villages, making it difficult to navigate the large vehicles around them and there were surprisingly thick forest areas that obstructed a lot of our visibility. The events of these first few days in Khan Neshin were a bit of a blur, but I do remember that we began taking enemy contact from various locations with small arms fire and indirect mortar fire very quickly. That was when I knew that things were for real. There were people who not only wanted us gone but were willing to fight with us and kill us. It is a feeling that's hard to describe because you picture the scenario often in your mind that when it happens, it seems totally surreal. This went on for the first few days with each of the four platoons taking contact at different times but sustaining no casualties. Most often it would be small arms fire from a distance followed by mortar rounds that were alarmingly accurate. You'd just be parked somewhere and out of nowhere, an explosion would occur a short distance away and it took a moment to realize that the intent was for that to land on top of you and kill you. It was enough to keep me on my toes and realize that the situation was serious but it also felt exciting and exhilarating because none of us had gotten hurt yet.

In the center of Khan Neshin was a large castle built of compacted sand and brick. It was an impressive sight with walls standing approximately 40 feet high and formed in a square with observation posts at each corner. It had a large opening at the front that looked like it should have had a massive door on it but was probably removed many years earlier. It looked very much like what I had always pictured a medieval castle to look like except it was made of mud and sand that appeared weathered from the hundreds of years of exposure to the sun and elements. It was overall an imposing sight. It was located at the highest point of elevation in the city center so it stuck out on the horizon and provided an overview of everything for miles around it. It was rumored to have been built in the 12th century and it certainly looked like it. It was decided that Charlie Company and the headquarters element would seize the castle and use it as a forward operating outpost, then hold it until Delta Company arrived to reinforce us and take over the castle so we could continue pushing south toward the Pakistan border. This sounded like an excellent idea and was at the time because you could view the entire battle area, but the problem was that the castle was also an excellent target for indirect mortar and rocket fire from the Taliban hiding in the area. We knew that this was inevitable if we set up there, but also knew that we could locate and kill the enemy with relative ease. We took the castle with ease as it was unoccupied by the locals who chose to live in the surrounding towns instead. As we first approached the castle, we had to drive through the narrow roads crowded with mud houses on both sides. As we made our way through the neighborhoods, the locals came out to stare at us from their rooftops. I could see the anger in their eyes and sensed that they were evaluating our equipment and strength as we passed. We all knew that many of these men staring at us would most likely be attacking us in the near future but there was nothing we could do about it until they made the first move. The castle then went on to take mortar or rocket fire every day for nearly 30 days from small Taliban teams that would set up their mortars and rockets, fire them, and then quickly leave the area before we could react. I recall one particular time when my crew and I were sitting down eating MRE (Meals Ready to Eat) and a rocket attack occurred. I had never heard anything so loud in my life. It sounded like a freight train going through the air and then crashed into the nearby ground causing an explosion of dust and flying debris. After the initial scare of the explosion wore off, the entire company was so pissed off and so excited that we all mounted our vehicles without being ordered to and began to leave the castle outpost to go find whoever shot the rockets. We made it to the front entry point when our company commander, Captain Connor, angrily told us to stand down. There was no point in leaving the outpost because our own mortars were already preparing to return fire on the area that our observation posts saw the attack come from. No one was hurt in the incident but it certainly made me realize how vulnerable of a position we were all in and how quickly a relaxing moment could turn into chaos.

Charlie Co. approaching the castle

Entrance to the castle.

My Gunner "Willie" in front of the castle.

During that time in early July, the pace of operations was so fast that I didn't have time to make entries in my journal. Many things happened during that time and I can remember vividly but cannot place a date on them. We were in multiple firefights and took various forms of enemy contact but sustained no wounded or killed. It was what I thought a real deployment to a combat zone would be like, I felt like we were in the Wild West. We were the southernmost element of the entire Marine Expeditionary Brigade and were handling combat operations on our own. We felt like we were taking the fight to the Taliban and winning every time. It was scary, exciting, and exhausting but I also felt that there was nowhere else in the world I'd rather be. It was everything that I had joined the Marines to do. I felt proud and knew that I was part of history unfolding in real time. I often thought about Nick and imagined that he was dealing with the same things if not worse. I knew the city of Garmsir was a well-known Taliban stronghold and they wouldn't give it up without a serious fight.

Patrolling the town of Khan Neshin

Sometime in early July 2009

I'm not sure what day it is in July and I don't really care to. Things have changed greatly. We came down south and we have had enemy contact every day since. Two days ago my guys and I had our turn. We were sitting on a berm all morning observing the north side of town. It was very hot and boring and we were all just waiting to leave. After a while four Afghans came to the canal in front of the berm to wash and smoke hash, I didn't think much of it at the time. When we got word to leave and started mounting up the four Afghans left immediately, I still did not think much of it. We left and went down the same road we came in on at the east side of a compound.

My vehicle was in the middle of five when three mortar rounds impacted, one hit not even 15 feet on my left flank and the concussion buckled me into the vehicle commander hole. I heard "incoming" on the radio and stayed down for a second, afraid that the next round would be right on top of my head. After I heard no explosion I got up and heard bullets cracking and whizzing past my head and hit all over my vehicle. I racked my 240 (mounted machine gun on movable turret connected to vehicle commanders hatch) back and opened fire, emptying 200 rounds in less than a minute at the compound. I then radioed up to Blue 1(platoons are labeled as different colors and the vehicles each have a number. Blue 1 was my platoon commander, Lt. Mahoney) requesting to be cleared hot on the TOW missiles because I could see the building where all the muzzle flashes were coming from. I was cleared hot. Willie (Chad Williams, my gunner and one of the most reliable people I've ever known) erected the turret and I got him on target and he fired with the missile impacting directly on the building, leveling half of it and killing whoever was inside. I wanted to be sure so I had him fire a second missile but it was a dud and launched it but never exploded. While all of this was happening I was still firing hundreds of 7.62 mm from my 240 at the compound. I would say I fired between 400-500 rounds. The barrel got so hot at that point that I stopped firing and grabbed the MK-12(a 5.56 mm M16 A2 with suppressor, 13X scope, and fully auto option) I had next to me and had Willie spotting targets with the TOW missile sights at targets still firing at us. There was a man in black shooting from an arched doorway that we both had eyes on so I got him in my sights and fired. We both saw the man fall to the ground and not get back up. I moved on to look for new targets and continued to engage with the 5.56 mm. After the TOW missile and all the fire we had returned, the fire coming at us greatly decreased. At this point our Bravo section and part of 3rd platoon had moved around the southern flank of the compound, so in fear of firing at friendly's I held off with the 7.62 mm and continued scanning with the MK-12 for targets. We sat outside the compound for another three hours or so trying to gather up women and children in the area and any non-combatant civilians who may have been wounded. We came to find out that the two remaining Taliban tried to flee by shooting off an old woman's hand and pretending she was their mother so they could slip past us, but the Marines searching them discovered the truth and they were detained. My whole life I wondered how I would handle a situation like that I thought maybe that I would freeze or panic in fear of my own life and all the guys under me but I didn't at all. I probably made over 50 key decisions in that time while returning fire myself and I'd say that most of them were off of reflex and instincts alone. I'm very proud of my crew and I think they've all proved themselves. The day after intel reported at least two dead Taliban in that compound.

That enemy contact in early July was the most significant contact that I encountered during the entire deployment. Everything prior to that had not been directed specifically at me but was more of a platoon or company engagement with various elements moving about and experiencing different parts of the fight. During those times, one vehicle may have been receiving enemy contact while another was simply hearing it on the radio from a distance and maneuvering to flank the enemy or get into support positions. This was the first time I felt I may actually be killed. It was a feeling that despite what I previously thought, I was not prepared for at 21 years old. I had never in my life felt fear that initially came on as nearly total panic to the point of my body freezing. It was so alarming to go from a mundane and boring day to being under such an intense attack that I felt myself go into a sort of tunnel vision that brought my focus solely to the idea that additional mortar rounds were going to land directly on top of me and I'd be dead at any moment. When the first rounds hit so close to my vehicle, my natural instinct was to duck down inside the vehicle. Once I got my bearings and realized that we were also getting shot at with small arms fire that I could hear pinging off the sides of the vehicle, I shifted my focus to standing up and shooting back. I felt that I had accepted the situation and wasn't going to be in a defensive position but instead fight back. I was pissed off at the idea that these people were trying to kill us. I mentioned my gunner Chad Williams in the journal entry, but the rest of my crew played just as important of roles. My driver Jake Tyrell maneuvered our vehicle perfectly while in the kill zone of a combined small arms and mortar attack. I can't imagine how confusing and scary it must have been to be inside of the confined driver's area as explosions were happening right next to the vehicle and bullets were pinging off of the thin armor. At least I had the ability to see and react to what was going on. I have no doubt that Jake wanted nothing more than to be outside and able to return fire, but he did his job and did it perfectly. My missile loader in the rear of the vehicle, Benjamin Cooke, performed outstandingly and between loading the two Two missiles, he returned small arms fire by exposing his body out of the back of the vehicle.

It felt like I didn't come down from the adrenaline rush of the firefight for several days. When we got back to the castle at the end of the day, we debriefed with the entire company and people were congratulating me for getting what we believed was the first confirmed kill when I engaged the dark figure I saw with the MK-12 and saw him fall. I'll never know if I actually killed anyone but at the time, it made me feel like I had accomplished something great. I had killed the enemy that was trying to kill us and I was proud of it. It's a strange thing to describe to someone who wasn't in that situation or environment why the idea of killing another human being is something you'd be proud of but in that context, it was the mentality of everyone there and had to be. Fifteen years later I still feel that the pride was justified and the idea of killing was necessary, but I feel that the reasons for getting to that point in the first place are wrong. I feel that all wars are civil wars because we are all citizens of the same planet and members of the human race. I understand that violence and conflict will forever be part of human nature and if I had to put myself in a similar situation again to protect the ones I love, I would but I believe that the value of human life should never be taken for granted. I remember calling my mom the next day on the company satellite phone to tell her that I was fine and not to worry. I asked her how the Fourth of July holiday was back home then told her, "We've been dealing with our own kind of fireworks but it's all good for us," then laughed to reassure her once again. I also asked if she had any updates on Nick and she told me that she had talked to his mother, Lisa, recently and that he was doing well too. While I was relieved to hear that Nick was still alive, I had also been hearing reports of how many casualties 2/8 was taking. I was concerned but put it in the back of my mind as best I could.

That enemy contact was completely and utterly insignificant in the grand scheme of the entire operation in Helmand Province. It was most likely insignificant to some of the other members of Charlie Company as well, who were not as directly involved. The fact is that it was extremely significant to ME. This was a turning point in my life, a moment where I faced fear and danger then reacted in a way that I felt proud of. Even 15 years later, I think about this series of events every day. A common thing amongst veterans is to compare their experiences to that of previous wars or battles and in the process, completely downplay the significance to themselves. People will think what they experienced is nothing compared to the Vietnam War, the people in Vietnam tell themselves it was nothing compared to the Korean War and the people in Korea think their experiences couldn't have been as bad as the World War 2 veterans and so on. The fact is that if something is a big deal to you, then it is a big deal.

This could be one firefight, one IED blast, one mortar attack. If it causes you trauma then that is all that matters. Comparing your experiences to that of another person does nothing to help you deal with your own but only minimizes them until they finally catch up with you.

A short time after those events, Charlie Company had moved out from the Khan Neshin castle and set up COP (**C**ombat **O**ut**P**ost) Payne. The location was selected for its strategic value as it overlooked the fish hook of the Helmand River and provided an overview of most of the battle area. The COP consisted of a large dirt berm built by engineers to form a circle with one guarded entrance in the front and rear and watch towers facing in every direction. The berm was approximately 10 feet high and had barbed wire on top of it as well as the overwatch stands. It was nothing more than a giant dust bowl approximately 200 meters wide where we parked our vehicles and set up a command post. It was also another ideal target for indirect fire, which we quickly found out. The rear gate faced south toward the Helmand River and allowed easy access for future crossings. The new COP was to be occupied by Charlie Company, while Delta Company who had recently arrived in Afghanistan to reinforce Charlie, stayed at the Khan Neshin Castle and maintained that battle space.

View of the Helmand River from the elevated area near COP Payne

In the process of securing the area for COP Payne to be built, Charlie Company was tasked with crossing the Helmand River. This was a big deal at the time because while the LAVs were considered amphibious vehicles, none of us had actually used them in water deeper than the tires. The Helmand River runs through the entire province and is the lifeline for agriculture and populated areas. Everything near the river is as green as the jungle but the further you get away from it, the surroundings become a barren desert. The river is as wide as two football fields in some places and as small as a stream in others. The area where we decided to cross was approximately 100 yards wide with what seemed like a mild current. The water was surprisingly clear and clean. This was because the locals made every effort not to pollute the river for its farming value and its use as the main source of drinking water. When the time came to cross the river, we were not entirely sure how the vehicles would perform or what the exact depths of the river were. For all we knew, we could have driven into the water and the vehicles would quickly begin taking on water until they sunk to the bottom and got stuck in the middle of the river. The crossing was exciting and luckily no issues arose. We all made it across safely and began to gain ground near the Pakistani border where the majority of the Taliban were getting their supplies and manpower from.

Charlie Co. crossing the Helmand River

We also used the river to bathe ourselves for the first time in quite a while. Elements of Charlie Company would set up security while others jumped in the water and swam around. It was a very fun time and a welcomed break from operations. What started out as a means to wash our disgusting bodies turned into a full-blown day at the beach. People were swimming around and having chicken fights with Marines on their shoulders while taking videos and pictures. It was a special time and one of my favorite memories from that deployment. It was also the first reminder in a long time that the majority of us were still just kids at heart, who when given the opportunity to swim and play in the water would gladly take it. I recall one time we were bathing in the river and had to cut it abruptly short because COP Payne, which was only a short distance away from the area we swam in, began taking mortar fire. The contrast of a bunch of 19-23- year-olds swimming in the river in our underwear and tossing each other off of our shoulders to mortar rounds intended to kill us landing a short distance away was a cold reminder that it was not a day at the beach. On July 11th, we were all gathered on the same beach area after swimming and I heard what was clearly some sort of explosion in the distance. I did not think much of it at the time, as those noises had become a common occurrence. That explosion became another pivotal turning point of that summer and a day I'd never forget.

Swimming in the Helmand River

Sometime Around July 13,

Still July, I think it't the 13th. We took our first casualties two days ago. The day started out with us returning from our trip across the river and doing vehicle maintenance in the morning. After that we got to go swimming in the Helmand River, which was really good because not only was it 120 degrees outside, but none of us had showered in two weeks. For that two hours of swimming I felt like I might as well have been home. Everyone was having fun and smiling and happy, No one knew that none of us would be smiling by the end of the day. We got out of the water and went back to the beach where our vehicles were and lounged around eating and getting more sun burned. As we were sitting there around dusk I heard a faint boom of an explosion but didn't think much of it. About five minutes later it came over the radio that one platoon was to get ready to go out while the other stood by to reinforce. Details of what was going on quickly started circulating. It turned out that Delta Company had a vehicle hit with an IED on a convoy on the way to COP Payne. Red platoon left to go secure the blast sight and we (blue platoon) followed shortly after. On our way out the MEDEVAC (medical evacuation by helicopter) was in process and we had to stop and back up to let the vehicles with the casualties on them go by us to get to the helicopter about to land. The MRAP (Mine Resistant Ambush Protected, a very large vehicle) carrying the casualties missed the turn and fell into a ditch next to it and was unable to get out. Gunny Washechecke ran out of his vehicle and I followed behind him to help pull the stretcher out. What I saw next I'll never forget for the rest of my life. I saw them pulling the stretcher out when I got there and started to help and I saw the man, who I later found out was Master Sergeant Jerome D. Hatfield, lying on the stretcher. His face was completely covered with bandages with an air tube coming out of his mouth. His legs were completely mutilated and destroyed. It just looked like chunks of white flesh with bones sticking out and bloody. Eight or so

Marines began carrying the stretcher to the landing helicopter and I returned to my vehicle. I felt sick to my stomach. A cold sense of reality set in along with the fact that it could be me in that stretcher any day now. We carried on with our mission to go recover the destroyed LAV. I later found out that the driver was still dead inside the vehicle. We sat there around the destroyed LAV in a coil until Red Platoon took over and we returned to base for the night. I found out that the other Marine killed was named Lance Corporal Pedro Barboza-Flores, who I had met but cannot say I really knew him. Everyone knew Master Sergeant Hatfield. He'd been in 2nd LAR as long as anyone could remember. He left behind a wife and three kids and was less than two years away from retiring. I have this deep sadness for them both that I don't think I'll ever lose.

Pedro Barboza-Flores, a kid who will never get to live life beyond the town of Khan Neshin Afghanistan. Master Sergeant Hatfield, who's wife will go on with no husband and who's kids will grow up with no father, and all of this for no reason that is clear to me or anyone else here. I'm not sure anymore how I'm going to be able to handle if any of my friends die here. I'm worried sick that Nick might be one of the seven Marines that died in Garmsir with 2/8. From what I've heard they are having a real tough time up there. So tough that they requested our company to go up there and help. The latest news is that we are going up north to help 2/8 in two or three days. I hope it's true, maybe I'll see Nick there or at least find out that he's alive. I don't think that either of us are ever going to be the same again after all this. I hope every one of my friends is enjoying the summer back home because they will never have the slightest idea of what goes on here and what it's like to know that you or your friends could die at any moment. I pray for the families of those men and pray that there will be no more casualties to come.

Jerome Hatfield

Pedro Barboza-Flores

After the first couple weeks in Khan Neshin, it became clear that the Taliban had very little intention of engaging us in what would be considered a traditional firefight. Our firepower and assets were simply too much for them to contend with, so they resorted to burying IEDs (Improvised Explosive Devices) anywhere they thought that our vehicles would travel or the patrols would walk. The IED that killed Master Sergeant Hatfield and Lance Corporal Barboza- Flores was the first one that made us realize how much of a threat they truly were. Prior to that, we had either located the IEDs before they exploded or were unaware of them because we had avoided them entirely. Their deaths raised the deployment to a new level of seriousness for us all. While the enemy engagements we had in the first two weeks were exhilarating and scary, I always felt that we had the upper hand. I knew that we would come out on top of any firefight with the exception of mortar or rocket rounds striking one of our vehicles or foot patrols. It just seemed to me that once the Taliban realized that we were not going to simply break contact and leave the area, they felt that they needed to change their methods and become ghosts on the battlefield. This meant that they would bury IEDs in the dark of night then hide during the day and observe the damage they created from a distance.

The effects of a medium-sized IED on an LAV-25

The psychological effect of driving around all day in a lightly armored vehicle, especially after it had been proven that the armor would not prevent a catastrophic kill, was extremely taxing. We took measures to avoid areas where we thought IEDs would be located, but at a certain point there was no choice but to take already established areas of travel due to the rough terrain. Engineers and Explosive Ordnance Disposal technicians did an amazing and courageous job of clearing IEDs but we all knew that we could not locate them all. It is also important to understand the reality of driving over an IED on a dusty dirt road in the desert. It is not a glorious event. It is not a large-scale battle with moving parts and a back and forth engagement that results in victory for one side and defeat for the other. It can be the most ordinary of days with not a single indication of enemy in the area or danger around. The explosion happens out of nowhere and the results are gruesome and chaotic. The lurking and invisible threat makes everyone feel that the only somewhat safe place is inside the confines of the combat outposts, which were still vulnerable to indirect mortar and rocket attacks. They create a helpless feeling of constant vulnerability that demoralizes troops who have little to no defense against them. At times it felt like you were playing a game of Russian roulette every time you drove through certain areas. It is truly one of the most terrifying parts of the wars in Afghanistan and Iraq and is talked about the least. In many ways, the manufacturing and implementation of improvised explosive devices came to define both conflicts in the later years.

We continued our daily patrols and operations while using COP Payne as our home base. We would leave in platoon or company-sized elements for several days then come back to rest, recover, and perform vehicle maintenance. We fell into what could be considered a routine for the conditions at the time, but there were always missions that arose and there was never any real set schedule. Due to our rapid mechanized mobility, our battle space was massive compared to traditional infantry units and because of that, there were still many areas we were patrolling for the first time. The enemy contact began to slow down a little by the middle of July with sporadic firefights and mostly indirect mortar fire targeted at COP Payne and the Khan Neshin Castle.

The castle took mortar fire nearly every day for the month of July and on July 23rd, Sergeant Ryan Lane of Delta Company was killed by a mortar round that landed inside the castle. He was 25 years old from Pittsburg, Pennsylvania and on his 2nd deployment to Afghanistan. I was not present during this incident and did not personally know Sergeant Lane but regardless, I still felt great sadness for the loss of his life. It was another reminder of how dangerous of a place we were in.

Ryan Lane

Most of July became a blur of days melting together in the hot summer sun. It is easy to completely lose track of time in such an environment when you have no contact with the outside world. So much of a deployment is either life-threatening danger and excitement or mind-numbing boredom. When the pace slows down, there is absolutely nothing to do but bullshit with your fellow Marines or be alone with your thoughts. Spending so much time around the same people with no outside distractions can become a challenge in itself. It's inevitable that people will butt heads at times but that's just an expected part of it all. The pace of operations was still exhausting and didn't seem to be slowing down any time soon, but we all started to feel that we were making progress in the area. The fact that the Taliban would only engage us with IEDs or indirect fire at least showed that they were afraid of us, and we felt a victory in itself from that fact.

THE TURNING POINT

On July 27th, I used the company's only satellite phone to call home and check in with my mom. I tried to do this as often as possible to let her know that I was alright in spite of the grim reports of U.S. casualties in the Helmand Province during that summer. Each time I called I would ask again if she heard anything about Nick since she was close friends with Nick's mother, Lisa, and spoke with her often. On this particular night, we had just gotten back from an operation across the Helmand River and were preparing to take several days off in order to repair our vehicles and equipment. The phone rang and my mom finally answered. When you call on a satellite phone, there is a delay because of the time it takes the signal to reach the satellite then bounce off and get to wherever you're calling. You speak and the person on the other end doesn't hear what you say for close to a full 10 seconds at times. I never thought about what time it was back home and Afghanistan time was 8.5 hours ahead of American east coast time, so my mom would receive calls at all hours of the day or night. I can't even imagine how stressful it must have been to sit around hoping that nothing prevented her from missing what could potentially be the last time she ever talked to her son. The first thing she said to me was, "Andrew? Has anyone contacted you?" I could hear fear and panic in her voice that I'd never heard and will remember for the rest of my life, something was very wrong. I said no, thinking that the question was absurd considering I was in the middle of the desert and my only contact with the outside world was the one satellite phone I was using to call her.

She then said to me, "Nick has been killed, he died on July 23rd." I refused to believe what I was hearing, as though the statement simply didn't register in my brain. I asked if she was sure about this and insisted that maybe he was only wounded, that maybe she had gotten wrong information and he was in a hospital somewhere with a recovery ahead of him. She then told me that he was killed by an IED. I do not recall any more details of the conversation after that other than my mother saying to me, "Andrew, I am so worried about you," while crying and barely keeping herself together. I don't remember what I said to reassure her or how the phone call ended. As hard as the situation was for me, at least I knew where I was and was somewhat in control of what I was doing and how I handled it. To her everything was a complete mystery where she had nothing but time to imagine the worst.

I was in a complete state of shock and disbelief. Nick or I being killed in this place was something I had thought about but in an almost abstract way that was totally out of the realm of possibility. I always thought it was something that happened to other people. It sounds so foolish to say, but part of me truly believed we were invincible. That all of this would be a story we'd be talking about for years to come. That casualties were part of combat, but we would not be one of them. We would mourn any friends we lost together and live our lives for them, tell stories about them, but live through these ourselves. We had joined the Marines together and were going to get out of the Marines together too. We planned on going to college and living the life we felt we had missed on to fulfill our dream of becoming Marines. This was not supposed to happen, I knew the reality of the situation we were in but I still felt that Nick and I were somehow protected from death despite seeing the evidence all around me that no one was.

It's hard to imagine the true reality of the casualties of the wars in Iraq and Afghanistan because such a small part of America was fighting in it. It wasn't something that affected the everyday person and most people weren't even aware of what was going on in either place, and especially Afghanistan which was in the midst of a huge offensive operation. Most people didn't even know that Iraq and Afghanistan were two different places nowhere near each other. I remember meeting some people who honestly believed that we were in Afghanistan because of oil, a statement so absurd but revealing to some of the American people's apathy toward the conflict. I once heard a saying used to describe the majority of the American people and their view on the wars: "America isn't at war, it's at the mall." It's not that I feel that America didn't care about these wars but they just weren't affected by them enough to care unless they were directly involved somehow. All the people that were there went voluntarily and most of them were happy to do so. Nick was the first person I truly knew to be killed in the war, a friend beyond the military who came from the same place I did. It was just too much to comprehend and rationalize in my mind.

Nick's death and the events surrounding it are not my story to tell. Many other people were involved and affected by the events of that day but I do not intend to attempt to retell the story because I was not there and had nothing to do with what transpired that day. I simply want to share my experience with Nick's death and everything that followed for me. Every single person involved in that day has their own story to tell and I cannot disrespect any of them by attempting to recount the events in a way that may not be entirely factual. What I can say for certain is that my friend Nick Xiarhos died from wounds suffered from an improvised explosive device on a dusty dirt road in a place called Garmsir in the Helmand Province of Afghanistan. A place that most people have never heard of and never will unless they were directly tied to the events that occurred in the summer of 2009. He died as a young man who volunteered to go fight for a country that he believed so strongly in that he would sacrifice his life for it. Wars are always terrible and you don't have to look far into the history of the United States to see that the causes for its wars are not always as clear as they initially seem, and the end results can be complicated and messy, but it is the fact that the youth are willing to go that matters. Nick embodied every aspect of the pride and fighting spirit of America. It's hard to imagine the heights he would have reached in his life after the Marine Corps. His possibilities were endless but were cut short at 21 years old because he volunteered to go to a place where he knew he could do some good and lead fellow Marines while serving a purpose far greater than himself. Nick died doing exactly what he wanted to be doing in the only place he wanted to be at that time.

Everything after that phone call became a blur to me. I called Nick's father, Steve, at one point but barely remember the conversation other than him telling me that Nick fought for his life for several hours before succumbing to internal wounds. I tried to assure him that we were taking the fight to the Taliban and that I'd get whatever revenge I possibly could but I knew that had no real meaning. I knew that nothing I could say or do could change anything for Nick's dad or make him feel better. Steve ended our conversation by telling me that the last thing Nick said when he called home was, "Don't worry about me, I'm living the dream."

I went back to my platoon as a complete mess. I told them what happened and couldn't contain my emotions. A terrible sand storm began to roll through the area and I spent the next two days in a make shift tent that I constructed from my poncho liner to shield me from the elements. At that time we had no tents on COP Payne and were sleeping on the ground outside of our vehicles. I cried in that makeshift tent and smoked cigarettes for longer than I remember. I simply didn't have the ability to cope with the reality of the situation at that age, in that place, and at that time. By then, the entire company was aware of my friend Nick being killed and checked on me but also gave me my space. I pulled myself together after a while and began writing a eulogy in my journal for Nick that I would transcribe to my mom over the satellite phone so that she could read it on my behalf at Nick's funeral since I thought there was no possible way I could attend.

I wrote the eulogy and accepted that I would be exactly where I was supposed to be for my friend's funeral in Afghanistan with my Marines. I then began the process of compartmentalizing everything so that I could effectively move on and be there for the guys who needed me. It was at that point in my life that I learned that my mental capabilities were far greater than I was aware of. I learned that I could bury something in my mind and lock it away when I needed to in order to accomplish what needed to be done. I could internalize or write about it in my journal, but I learned the ability to remain composed on the outside. While that is not the best long-term solution to deal with traumatic events, it is necessary at times in life. I kept this method up for many years after my time in the Marines before I was able to embrace the fact that being vulnerable is a strength, not a weakness. That it was okay to get help when I needed and admit when I was struggling. It was even more difficult during this time for me because our operational pace had slowed down significantly as we were attempting to get some much needed rest and repair vehicles and equipment. At a time when I desperately needed distractions, it was hard to find them.

I continued to call my mom as often as possible to get updates on what was happening back home and to ease her mind about my current situation. I also spent a lot of time with the battalion Chaplin, Lt. Rivers. He was invaluable during those times with the spiritual guidance he provided. I was never the type of person to go to church or practice religion, but I found a form of spirituality that was my own and that I'd build upon later in life. After a couple days had passed, my platoon commander, Lt. Mahoney, and Company commander, Captain Connor, came to me and said that the battalion commander wanted to see me in his tent. This would normally be a strange request, but considering the entire company knew about Nick's death and how much it meant to me, I assumed he wanted to talk to me about that. Lt. Col. Grattan was also a Massachusetts native so I'm sure the situation hit close to home for him as well. I entered his tent at night and he began to tell me how sorry he was to hear about Nick's death. The man had a command presence that I'll never forget. The way he spoke seemed so confident like you'd expect an infantry battalion commander to sound, but with a tone of sincerity and assurance that instantly calmed me. He was a true leader and I respected him greatly. He then asked me a question that completely blindsided me. He looked at me with the serious look of a Marine Corps Lieutenant Colonel and said, "How would you feel about going home to attend his funeral?" My immediate reaction was to tell him that I didn't feel that it was an option because I was a vehicle commander and my Marines needed me, and that I wouldn't feel right leaving them. I felt that the very idea of leaving that place was so morally wrong that to even entertain it was a violation of a silent code we'd all adopted as Marines, to not leave each other behind. He said that he understood and respected my position but assured me that the company was going into a 10-day period of rest and recovery while it awaited orders for a future operation north of our position. He assured me that I'd miss nothing of any significance and that my Marines would be fine. I asked him repeatedly if the operational break was a sure thing and if the orders could change while explaining that I couldn't live with myself if something happened while I was gone. He assured me it was the plan and I believed and trusted him. I knew he wouldn't steer me wrong or suggest this option if he didn't know exactly what he was talking about. I was so caught up in the surprise of the question itself that I never thought to ask how it would even be possible, considering that we were the southernmost element of the entire operation and basically in the middle of nowhere. Lt. Col. Grattan then went on to tell me that he had received a call from the commander of the entire MEB, Brigadier General Nicholson, telling him to give me the option to go home to attend Nick's funeral. This was extremely confusing to me at the time, and he seemed just as surprised by the request as I was. Regardless of the weight that the General's influence had, he assured me that the decision was still mine to make but that I had to make it right then because a helicopter would be at our outpost the following morning to take me to Camp Leatherneck. I asked again for his reassurance that the company would be on a break from operations while I was gone and he told me not to worry. I then told him that I would be getting on that helicopter the next morning to start the long journey to Cape Cod, Massachusetts, from the southernmost element of a massive military operation near the border of Pakistan.

I felt incredibly overwhelmed by the entire situation and the range of emotions I was experiencing. I also felt a strong sense of shame for leaving my guys and the rest of the company after everything we'd been through and everything that was still to come. I knew Marines who had children born while they were deployed and were unable to see them or be there for their wives. Why should I be able to go home and not them? It all felt so wrong. I still carry a tremendous amount of guilt and shame to this day for making that decision to leave my Marines. It was one of the most conflicting and difficult decisions I've ever had to make. I knew in my heart how broken and scared Nick's family and my entire community back home were, and I felt that going home and being there could possibly make some small difference to people. I felt that reading the eulogy I wrote at his funeral might give everyone some small sense of peace or reassurance. I also knew that I could answer questions people had about what was really going on in Afghanistan.

I was still incredibly confused as to how Brigadier General Nicholson, who oversaw the entire military operation in the Helmand Province, got involved in this at all. Nick was one of many tragic casualties that summer and I highly doubted that he was sending out orders like this regularly, or even at all. I decided to use the satellite phone to call my mom and discovered exactly how that happened. My mom told me that one of my high school class mates, Nicole Warren, graduated and went on to intern in some way for Senator John Kerry or worked closely with his office and he was the one making this happen. She said that Nicole had told him the story and Senator Kerry coordinated everything else somehow. My mom didn't know many more details but that explanation was enough for me at the time. In the process of writing this, I reached out to Nicole and she gave me more details about exactly how that chain of events occurred. After high school, Nicole began interning for Rhode Island Senator Jack Reed's office. When Nick was killed, she called him and told him the story and that I was still in Afghanistan as part of the same operation. Senator Reed then told her that he would see what he could do to get me home. Senator Reed then called his friend Senator John Kerry to ask for help.

Senator Kerry said that he had friends killed in the Vietnam War and was unable to attend their funerals, so he would do whatever he could to get me home to say goodbye to my friend. The two senators then made a phone call to the Secretary of Defense, Robert Gates, who then sent the orders down the chain of command that resulted in Lt. Col. Grattan receiving a phone call from Brigadier General Nicholson. The orders for me to go home ultimately came from the Secretary of Defense, the commander in chief of the entire United States armed forces who reports directly to the President of the United States. In the process of writing this story, I also reached out to Lt. Col. Tim Grattan to ask him more about how he had received the orders to get me home. We corresponded through email and he told me that Brigadier General Nicholson had called him directly and told him the specifics of the story and how the General felt it was imperative that I get home to say goodbye to my friend Nick. Tim Grattan told me, "Sending you to accompany Nick home was never a question of if, it was a question of when and how."

The next morning, a helicopter arrived at COP Payne and I got on it with few of my belongings. We then flew to Camp Leatherneck where I was told that I would be getting on another helicopter the next morning that would take me to Bagram Air Base. I used the time at Camp Leatherneck to stuff my face at the chow hall. Up until then my diet consisted of MREs, cigarettes, and caffeine whenever I could get it. The next morning I flew to Bagram where I met with a Marine liaison whose job was to coordinate commercial flights for anyone leaving or coming back into Afghanistan. I didn't receive exact orders from my battalion commander on when to be back, so I was not sure what to tell the Marine about a return flight. I knew that I didn't want to be home for more than a week so I told him seven days. He printed my tickets and told me that I would be getting on a C5 military plane to fly to Germany, where I would then get on a commercial airliner to head to America. My only document to get back into Afghanistan was a return flight ticket voucher. So much of this time is a blur to me now. The contrast of going from COP Payne near the Pakistan border to basically hitchhiking my way to the United States was stressful and overwhelming. Bagram Air Base was a completely different world. It was so established that it looked like a base in the United States. You would have no idea that there was a war going on if you were stationed at the base and the people there acted like that. Everyone I interacted with had a neat and clean uniform on and seemed totally unaware of what was happening in the Helmand Province at that time while also seeming not to care in the least.

Later that day I was shown where the airfield I needed to be at was to get on the C5 and was told to hang around the officers' chow hall. The chow hall was full of pilots and they were some of the coolest people I met the entire time I was in the military. I told them my situation and they explained to me exactly what would happen going forward and when the plane was going to leave. We eventually boarded the plane and I was surprised to see that the giant C5 aircraft was empty. A C5 is a massive cargo plane that can have multiple tanks inside of its cargo bay and is primarily used for the transport of heavy equipment. It was only me and the pilots taking the flight. They showed me an area near the cockpit where I could sit or lay down for the flight that would take several hours. I set myself up and put in my headphones to try to sleep. A C5 aircraft is incredibly loud the entire time you're on it, and taking a long flight on one is not a pleasant experience.

I arrived at Frankfurt Airport in Germany on July 29th and was met by another liaison who directed me to the terminal where my commercial flight home would be departing from. I was to get on an overnight flight that night that would fly me directly to Pease Air Force Base in Portsmouth, New Hampshire, which is also an airport for civilian international flights. While I waited for my flight, I called my mom to update her on my whereabouts and approximate arrival back in the United States. She told me that Nick's wake was going to be held on July 30th at Dennis-Yarmouth Regional High School, where Nick and I had graduated in 2006. The funeral was to be on July 31st, starting at the Greek Orthodox Church in Barnstable and ending at the National Cemetery in Bourne. It was decided that my dad would pick me up at the airport with my two childhood friends and also close friends of Nick's, P.J. McGlynn and

Brendan Walker. My mom wanted to be with Nick's family to support them and help coordinate whatever needed to be done. I got on the civilian-filled commercial airliner in my desert camouflage uniform because it was the only thing I had to wear at the time. I then tried to catch up on some sleep and clear my mind after the whirlwind of events I'd been through in the last 72 hours. It was still hard to comprehend that I wasn't in Afghanistan and even more difficult to wrap my mind around the fact that I was going home for Nick's funeral. I had not been home or seen my family since April.

NICK'S FUNERAL

I arrived at Pease Air Force base on the morning of July 30th. The plane touching down on American soil in itself was a remarkable event to me. It was something that I had envisioned and looked forward to for months but not under those circumstances. I felt excited for a brief moment but then sad for the reason why I was coming home and guilty for leaving my Marines. I got off and went into the busy airport and was totally overwhelmed by my surroundings in contrast to what they had been for the last few months. People were hurriedly walking about while I was in a daze from being in Afghanistan near the Pakistan border less than 72 hours earlier. I made my way to the arrivals area and found my dad parked and waiting with P.J. and Brendan who had followed him in their own car. My parents had gone through a terrible divorce as a result of my father having an affair when I was around 13 years old, and it greatly affected my relationship with him. So much of why I had joined the Marines in the first place was because he was in the Navy in his youth and I was fascinated by everything about the military since I was a small child. I remember watching the movie Saving Private Ryan with him and all I wanted after that was to be a soldier. My childhood consisted of playing with toy soldiers, dressing up as a soldier, and watching every war movie I could. The man faced his own battles that I'll never truly know about and unfortunately, his method of dealing with whatever demons he had was alcohol. He was never a bad man, only absent from my life because he felt it was too hard to face the reality of what he created with the divorce and the collateral damage it caused his kids. Later in life I came to realize that he was only a man just like me and I felt a deep sadness for him and wondered what his life could have been if he had done things differently. Since he was so absent from my life in any meaningful way, he had little involvement in any aspect of my time in the Marines, so for him to be the first person I saw during such an emotional and traumatic time was difficult. I still loved my father and was happy to see him, but I just wanted to be in that moment and not think about anything from the past. The fact that P.J. and Brendan were there gave the situation a much-needed relief. I got in the car with my dad and we began the two-and-a-half hour drive back to Cape Cod. They had the foresight to know that the first thing I'd want was a beer so they brought a 30-pack of Budweiser with them. I drank beer the whole car ride back to calm my nerves and was excited because I hadn't had a beer in five months. At the time it was the most delicious thing I'd ever tasted. I cannot remember what we talked about on that car ride beyond what I had been doing in Afghanistan. Because of my dad's minimal involvement in my life at that point, he did not even know Nick. Despite all of that, he was there to support me and I truly appreciated it. Since I had not drank in five months, I got a strong buzz going on the ride home and felt good. As we got closer to Cape Cod I could see signs on overpasses with Nick's name on them. It came as a stark reminder of the reality of why I had come home. Of course I had not forgotten, but I had gotten so caught up in the excitement of being back in the United States and the buzz I had going from the beers that I became distracted for a short time.

Once we crossed the Sagamore Bridge to enter Cape Cod, the signs and displays for Nick were incredible. The entire population of Cape Cod had come out to support Nick's family and show their respect and gratitude for the sacrifice he made. As we got closer to the high school where the wake was held, I began to see police cruisers from every department lining the roads, a massive American flag hung by a fire truck ladder over the street, and people of all demographics standing outside with American flags. It was truly breathtaking and I will never forget the support that the community showed during that time. I was overwhelmed with emotions after seeing how many people actually cared about what we were doing in Afghanistan and believed in the cause of defending the ideals and freedoms of America. It made me realize something else in that moment as well. As I saw the gathering of people showing support for Nick, I became aware of just how precious every single life lost in Iraq, Afghanistan and all of America's wars are. When you are not directly affected by one of these deaths, they may seem like only numbers that are periodically updated as the wars drag on, but to see the aftermath of a single life lost and the thousands of people affected by it makes you start to think about how every single person killed in any war has their own story. They had a family, friends, and communities that looked up to them as heroes. I thought of how this very same thing was happening in the hometowns of Master Sergeant Jerome Hatfield, Lance Corporal Pedro

Barboza-Flores, and Sergeant Ryan Lane. The entire scene made me ask myself, was what we were doing worth all of this? Did I even know why we were in Afghanistan anymore beyond the vague reason that we were fighting the global war on terrorism? It was hard not to have those thoughts when I saw the amount of sadness caused by Nick's death to my community and to think how many other communities were dealing with the same. I answered that question right then to myself and stand by that answer to this day. It didn't matter what the reasons were that we were in Afghanistan. What mattered was the fact that there were young men like Nick who would go where their country asked them to go without question to fight so that others didn't have to.

The procession for Nick approaching the high school

We pulled into the rear parking lot that led to the gym entrance where Nick's coffin was displayed. I was still in the same Marine desert camouflage uniform that had sand on it from wearing it three days earlier in Afghanistan. Normally, a Marine isn't supposed to wear camouflage uniforms in public or to any kind of event; it is the uniform regulation to wear the famous dress blue uniform or dress Alpha uniform, but I had no other option at the time and wanted to represent the Marine Corps in some way. I also had no other clothes of any kind available or the time to get them. I got out of the car and immediately began looking for my mom and Nick's little brother Alex, twin sisters Lizzie and Ashlynne, mother, and father. Everyone nearby began approaching me. It was unknown to me at the time but everyone knew the story of how I had gotten home from Afghanistan to attend Nick's wake and funeral. There were thousands of people at the high school and the scene was so overwhelming that I almost couldn't handle it. I entered the gym and found my mom, my sister Lynsey, and my brother Jon. I went up to my mom who hugged me and began crying a mixture of tears of joy that I was home and deep sadness for the reason why. I sank into that moment of my mom hugging me and felt like a little kid again. There was so much love in that moment that it's difficult to put into words. My mom had expected me to come home in November with Nick and under very different circumstances. When Nick and I previously returned from Iraq close to the same time, it was a big party for both of our families. Everyone was excited and celebrated while Nick and I talked about our deployments with pride. This wasn't how I was supposed to be coming home. I wasn't supposed to be home at all, the entire scene was so surreal that it felt like a dream that I'd wake up from in my sleeping bag in Afghanistan.

Reuniting with my mom and sister Lynsey at Nick's wake

It seemed like the entire population of Cape Cod was at the high school that day. There were so many people I cared about and wanted to give my attention to, but I was just too overwhelmed by the enormity of that moment. I found Nick's mom, Lisa, and hugged her. I embraced her and let her hold onto me for as long as she needed to. I then went to Nick's dad,

Nick being guarded by two Marines while the community pays their respects.

Steve, who was dressed proudly in his Yarmouth Police dress uniform, and hugged him. I could see the deep sadness on his face as he held his emotions together for his family and the people looking up to him. I felt that I could not cry in front of anyone. Not out of a distorted sense of pride or ego but because I felt that I needed to hold myself together for the people that couldn't. I felt that I was a walking representation of Nick and that everyone was looking to me for strength and guidance. Even if that may not have been true, that's how I felt at the time and how I wanted to conduct myself in that moment. I then hugged Nick's little brother, Alex, and his little teenage twin sisters, Ashlynne and Lizzie. The entire wake is mostly a blur to me to this day. The moment of my arrival was at the busiest part of the ceremony with the largest crowd possible and it felt like an out-of-body experience. The fact that I was also in the combat zone in Afghanistan not even three days earlier added another layer of emotions and confusion to the moment. The sadness of the situation and the excitement to see people I had not seen in many months was extremely difficult to balance. I still could not fully believe that my friend Nick was dead. That became a reality for me when I saw Nick's coffin on display draped in an American flag and surrounded by flowers. My friend was in that coffin, he was home from Afghanistan but in a way I never thought possible.

I once heard it said that there are countless versions of ourselves because every person you meet has their own perspective on who you are. Nick meant so much to so many different people, and every version of him that was ever encountered was loved. He was the most popular kid in high school, and not in an arrogant or cocky way, he was just kind to everyone. He was a leader in everything he did. He brought everyone around him up and had a way of calming a situation that made you feel like everything would be just fine. It's no coincidence that people like Nick are the ones who are killed in wars. This is because people like Nick take on responsibility that puts them in harm's way. They do the things that most others avoid and wait for someone else to handle. People seem to have a misconception that the Marine Corps is full of star athletes and studs, but this is not true. In many ways it is the land of misfit toys. Young men trying to prove themselves, find themselves, or escape from a past that they feel no longer serves them. A good portion of the Marine Corps is full of people attempting to blend in and not ruffle any feathers. Nick was not that type of Marine, he was the kind that rose to the top in anything he did. He continuously put himself in leadership roles and that carried with him into Afghanistan. Nick was new to 2/8 when they deployed because he had just transferred from his previous unit of 1/9. To go into that environment and be immediately put into a leadership position in a platoon that had been training together to deploy for months is a very difficult thing to do and it speaks volumes to Nick's attributes as a leader that he was able to do it. I know that any U.S. service member killed in combat would have received the same support from the communities of Cape Cod, but I felt that the difference that Nick made in his short time on earth attributed to the vast number of people attending and showing support. He was truly one of a kind.

Nicholas Xiarhos

I walked around the high school gymnasium talking to people and absorbing all that I could for what felt like hours. I took pictures with friends from high school and answered any questions I was asked about my time in Afghanistan and when I'd be going back. After the wake, I went back to my mom's house and immediately took off my uniform and got in the shower. I stood under the hot water for close to an hour. I felt like all the pores on my body had sand in them still from Afghanistan. I sat down on the ground and cried quietly to myself as I tried to comprehend everything I had been through in the last three days. I was home but none of it felt right. I was not excited about any of it. I felt guilty and ashamed for leaving my Marines in Afghanistan despite what my battalion commander told me about the operational stand down in my absence. I felt guilty and ashamed that I was there, alive and well, while my friend Nick was in a coffin on display for everyone to see. I felt guilty and ashamed of the spotlight that was on me for being home and the attention I was getting because of Nick's death. I felt guilty and ashamed for simply being alive. It was a terrible feeling at the time but I allowed myself that time in the shower to process it the best I could. At 21 years old, I simply did not have the tools to manage those emotions and the enormity of the situation I was facing. I wish I could say that I took that time to compose myself and move forward in a way that was productive and helpful to my mental state, but that isn't the truth. Instead what I did was drink, and drink, and drink, and drink, and then drink some more. I drank and told my friends and family stories about what had happened so far in Afghanistan. I remember standing in my mom's kitchen surrounded by family and friends and drunkenly telling stories about firefights, rocket attacks, and IEDs as though they'd have the slightest comprehension of what I was talking about. It was such a surreal thing to be abruptly removed from that Afghanistan environment and be thrust into the civilian world and home with my family and friends. I drank and partied with my close friends who were home from college and had all come together to mourn Nick. Every activity I did during that time involved heavy amounts of drinking.

The next morning on July 31st, 2009, I woke up hungover, put my desert camouflage uniform back on and prepared for Nick's funeral. I went to the high school with my mom where the funeral procession would begin and would ultimately bring Nick to his final resting place in the Bourne National Cemetery. A friend from high school and fellow Marine named Matt Medeux met me there in his dress blues uniform and offered to drive me in his truck for the procession. Matt was with 1st battalion 6th Marines down on Camp Lejeune and had done two serious deployments to Iraq and Afghanistan as well. He was on deployment in the summer of 2008 to Helmand Province, where my friends came back and told Nick and I about the realities of Afghanistan. He had been to the same city of Garmsir where Nick was killed. He knew what I had just been through so it was a huge relief and comfort to have him there with me. He knew Nick well but had also lost Marines on his own deployments and understood the process of what was going on. The funeral procession started off and the streets were lined with people showing support. There were American flags being waived as far as the eye could see and police, fire, and military vehicles lined the streets for what seemed like the entire drive.

The procession made its way to the Greek Orthodox Church in Barnstable, the town directly next to Yarmouth. We arrived and there were hundreds of people in the parking lot and entire police departments and Marines in uniform lined up in drill formations. I got out of Matt's truck and found my mom then began walking in the church past the rows of police officers, Marines, and other service members saluting. I got into the church and was directed to sit toward the front near Nick's family. As I was approaching the seats, I saw one of the men who was responsible for me being there, Senator John Kerry. I approached him and told him who

I was and thanked him for what he had done for me. We shook hands and had a brief conversation. I cannot recall exactly what was said, but I do remember the somber and understanding look on his face that said more than any words could in that moment. I then went to my seat and sat next to my mom. She handed me a printed copy of my eulogy so that I had it for when I got up to read it in front of the entire church. I had thought about that moment a few times but the gravity of it did not fully sink in until I was in the church and she handed me that paper. At that moment, I knew I had a chance to make a difference for all these people. Everyone there knew my story and the remarkable way I'd made it home just in time to be there. They knew that I was in the same area of Afghanistan as Nick, and that I'd be going back there very soon. I'd hoped that the words I spoke could lift everyone's spirits for even a brief moment.

I sat through the Greek Orthodox service and felt no nervousness or fear for my upcoming eulogy. I knew what I needed to do and felt as though my entire life had led to that moment in time. I thought about every attribute in Nick that I aspired to be like and how he would have handled the situation if it were me killed instead of him. I remembered every moment where he made a tough situation seem calm and manageable. I was as ready as I would ever be. The priest finished and informed the crowd that I would be reading a eulogy. I walked up to the altar and looked out at the crowd of people gathered in that church and could feel every single person's eyes fixated on me as an eerie sense of silence took over the room. I pulled out the paper and began reading without hesitation as I felt strangely at peace with the moment. I knew what my intention was and the impression I wanted to leave on everyone in the church. All I wanted was to make Nick's family, friends, and loved ones feel better for a brief moment, to make some sense of the sadness and chaos. I read the words on the page with confidence and even made sure to make light of some of the more comical parts about Nick and I's old party antics. I spoke from the heart and felt that I did my best.

Eulogy For Nick

Nick was my best friend, he was a fellow Marine, and was like a brother to me. In fact I think we were closer than most brothers could ever be. We'd experienced things together no one else could ever relate to unless they were there in that one moment in time. For the last four years of my life after high school everything I've done or experienced has been with Nick. I've had some of the funnest times of my life and I think a lot of that had to do with the deep love and appreciation we both shared for life due to the hardships and bitterness we shared that in the end can only make you do just that, love life. I can remember times when Nick and I would just sit in the barracks and down a whole handle of vodka or Jack Daniels and just talk and laugh and be happy we could both be sitting there and not in the damn desert. I can still remember the day we arrived at Parris Island, it seems like a lifetime ago, and how in the first week we got separated and Nick went to 2nd Battalion because he needed to be evaluated for his allergy to bees. I remember with a week left to go I broke my hips and had to have surgery and stay in the hospital for two months. As soon as Nick's graduation ceremony was over he came to the hospital to visit me. It's things like that I think that made us closer than any friends could ever be. Once we both got to the fleet it was every single weekend from Friday to Sunday that we would party non stop, and that's the way it should have been for two kids our age dealing with the things we were. Then we both went to Iraq in 2008, me with 2nd LAR and Nick with 1/9. I heard about the suicide bomber that hit a combat outpost near 1/9 about a month into the deployment and I prayed to god that Nick was alright. Luckily we had internet access at the time so I heard from him pretty quickly and my mind was put at ease. We both came home in October and picked up right where we left off, both better and wiser for the experiences we shared. As soon as we got back there was already talk of 2nd LAR deploying to Afghanistan before the summer came. That turned out to be Charlie Company and I got picked to go. So of course after I told Nick he wasn't going to let me go alone and he transferred to 2/8 to leave at the same time. We met up at Camp Leatherneck in Afghanistan where we hung out and waited to go down south. We saw each other on a regular basis there and just talked about how much it sucked and how we couldn't wait to get out in 2010. We pushed south on June 28th and that was the last I ever saw or heard from Nick. I don't think that either of us really knew what to expect here. The first week down in the Helmand Province was the craziest thing I've ever experienced. I don't think I can count on both hands the number of times I thought I was going to die. I knew Nick had to be going through the same and every chance I got I'd call home and ask if my mom had from Nick's mom. As casualties increased all across Helmand Province, including my own battalion, I couldn't help but constantly worry. On the evening of July 27th I called home to put my mind at ease again after hearing of another Marine in 2/8 being killed. My mom answered the phone and asked if anyone had contacted me and I instantly knew. I felt sick to my stomach. How could this happen to Nick? I thought we were both invincible, that all of this would just be drunk stories to tell when we got home. How could my friend I'd shared so much with and had so many future plans with after the Marine Corps be gone just like that? As I sit in here in a city called Khan Neshin in the Helmand Province of Afghanistan I keep asking myself these questions and I'm finding it very hard to sleep at night knowing the grief and mourning everyone is going through for my friend and fellow Marine. I wish more than anything in the world that I could be there for the service but it is impossible. Hopefully my mom reading this can help in some way to put everyone's hearts and minds at ease. I will end this with a quote from the most decorated soldier who ever lived and someone I find inspiration in, "We must never allow ourselves to forget the few men who went, and would go again to hell and back to preserve and defend what this country truly believes to be right and decent."

I finished reading the words I had written for Nick while sitting in that sandstorm in Afghanistan a week earlier, with no thought of ever being in this position to read them in front of all these people. I stood there and remembered everything that I had been through up until that point and that I'd be returning to that same place in a short while. I knew that I had to say something more to comfort everyone. As I looked out at the faces in the crowd, I focused on my mom and Nick's family. I then said the only thing that I could think of at that moment that could make them feel even the slightest bit of reassurance. I said sternly and boldly to the crowd, "The Taliban may have killed Nick, but I promise you all that we have killed many more of them and are going to continue to kill more until the job is done." At that time, my 21-year-old mind fresh from a combat zone, felt that this was the best thing to say in a Greek Orthodox Church in front of priests and even a United States Senator. In hindsight, I'm not sure how it landed with certain people but at the time, I did not care and I truly meant it. I could see people's reaction to that statement and could feel their enthusiasm at the thought of justice and vengeance being served to the enemy in Afghanistan that had taken Nick from them. While all those people may not wish death on another human being, the idea of it in the context of war is something that most people can understand. I feel that the fact that I was still in my Marine desert uniform, fresh from the battlefield of Helmand Province, and proudly delivering that message on that platform was the proudest moment of my life and still is. I felt that I was there for my friend Nick when he needed me in that moment. It was the last thing that I could do for him before he was forever buried. I learned that day that I would never let a moment or situation be bigger than myself. I would take what I learned from that experience and keep it for the rest of my life as a reminder of what I'm capable of when tested.

The service at the church concluded and everyone began to file out and get back into their vehicles to begin the journey to Nick's final resting place in the Bourne National Cemetery. The streets were lined with people showing their support for the entire slow-moving procession. Very little was said as Matt and I drove in his truck in a line of vehicles that stretched for as far as the eye could see. I knew that this next part was going to be the most difficult of all, to see Nick lowered into the ground amongst veterans of all of America's wars in front of everyone who ever loved him. One thing that I have learned over time is that it can be manageable for me to deal with my own trauma and pain in the moment. I can compartmentalize my feelings when I need to, but to see others that I love in physical or emotional pain is extremely difficult for me.

The procession arrived at the cemetery and made its way to Nick's grave site. A much smaller crowd of people was allowed at the cemetery compared to the wake and church service. Matt and I decided to go off to the side and stand with the other Marines as we waited for Nick's coffin to be brought forward on a horse-drawn carriage. The Marine Corps Hymn was sung loud and proudly as it was loaded onto the carriage and slowly made its way to the grave. We all stood at attention and saluted as Nick passed by us. I felt as though I was barely holding myself together at that point. I could see Nick's sisters crying and his brother, mother, and father standing still in a state of disbelief and exhaustion from everything that had led to that point.

When the singing stopped, the silence was unbearable. You could feel the emotions of pain and sadness in the air all around you.

A detail of Marines placed Nick's coffin on top of the grave and a Marine Corps band member with a bugle began to play the ceremonial Taps song that is customary for any fallen service member. I had heard that song many times in my life as it was played on Camp Lejeune every evening at sundown per Marine Corps tradition, but this was different. As

I stood there saluting, I could feel myself starting to lose composure. The enormity of the situation and everything I had been through for the last four months and last three days of travel began to catch up with me. The flag draped over Nick's coffin was then folded into the customary triangle and handed to Nick's mother and father by a Marine in dress blues. Once Taps concluded, everyone in attendance was given a rose to place on top of Nick's coffin as a final goodbye.

Nick's father then approached the coffin that his oldest son lay inside, his son who was still in high school only three years earlier with the dream of becoming a United States Marine.

He removed his cover and marched proudly forward in his police dress uniform with the rose in his hand. He knelt down, placed the rose on top of the coffin and stared at the coffin for a moment. He then slightly nodded his head and softly pounded the coffin with his fist three times before standing up and walking away. There were more roses placed on Nick's coffin before my turn came but what stuck with me to this day were Steve's actions. His nod of acknowledgment he made to himself at the reality of the situation before saying goodbye to his son with three pounds of his fist on that coffin. The mixture of sadness and pride that Nick's family felt in that moment is something that I cannot imagine.

Steven Xiarhos

When my turn came to place a rose on Nick's coffin, I approached slowly with Matt by my side. With each step I felt myself unraveling but desperately tried to hold myself together. I got to the coffin and placed the rose on top of it. I removed my cover and knelt down beside it and stared blankly in disbelief for a moment. Nick wasn't supposed to die; we were supposed to come home together and get out of the Marines then go to college. He was supposed to live a long life full of adventure and love. Nick would have gone on to do great things in the world but instead he was in that coffin in front of me, about to be lowered into the ground forever. I couldn't handle it. I finally broke down for the first time. I put my head into my hands and cried while I knelt in front of that coffin. I felt like I couldn't catch my breath and that I might pass out. I gave myself that moment to let out what I needed to then said not goodbye to him, but until we meet again.

I stood up and walked back over to the other Marines in formation as the remaining roses were placed by Nick's loved ones on his coffin. After the ceremony was concluded, I found my mom and stayed as close to her as I could. I knew she was imagining what it would be like if it were me instead of Nick inside that coffin. I'm sure she was also thinking about the fact that it was still a possibility that I could be killed in the same fashion when I returned to Afghanistan in the coming week. As hard as the entire situation was for me, I cannot imagine what she endured. At least I knew what to expect and what was happening on a daily basis because I was the one living it. Every day for her must have been a roller coaster of worry and emotions about me. She is the strongest woman I have ever met in my life and I don't know what I would have done without her support during that time.

As I prepared to leave the cemetery, a reporter from the Cape Cod Times found me and asked if I would be willing to do a short interview. I agreed and spoke with him on the road near Nick's grave. He asked me to tell him about Nick and I replied, "He was a great friend and an outstanding Marine, you see the turnout here. There are thousands of people and everybody loved him. I miss him a lot." He then asked me what thoughts were going through my head as I prepared to go back to Afghanistan after attending Nick's burial. I replied by saying, "I'm ready to go back to my Marines and get into the fight. It's what Nick would want, it's what I have to do, and we're going to kill as many of them as we can." He then asked how I felt about the Cape Cod community and the support it showed throughout everything and I said, "It's phenomenal, the turnout blows my mind. The whole Cape just lined up waiting for Nick's arrival." The reporter was respectful with his approach and I honestly appreciated his desire to hear my input at that time. I knew he was coming from a good place, and he was not trying to steal an emotional moment for a news story. I sensed that he cared as much about Nick's death as the rest of the Cape Cod citizens who had come out to show support. I also viewed it as another opportunity to hopefully make a difference and ease people's minds in some small way by ensuring that the Marines in the Helmand Province were taking the fight to the Taliban in every way possible.

At the time I felt that the only thing I could do was continually emphasize the idea that the Marines in Afghanistan were going to kill the Taliban. That they may have killed Nick, but they'd pay dearly for it. Was that true? I didn't think it mattered at the time, but I knew we were fighting ghosts over there. People who would bury homemade bombs in the ground during the night and then hide during the day to watch the gruesome results of their creations with satisfaction. It was a tough way to fight the enemy. While we certainly were killing them in great numbers all over the Helmand Province, it wasn't in the conventional idea of a war that most imagined. We'd get attacked from a distance and respond by calling in artillery on the entire area or dropping a 500-pound bomb. The Taliban were no match for the mighty American military, but they had no intention to ever stop fighting us. There was no way to "win" the fight over there because there was no clear definition or tangible concept of what victory would look like. The Taliban would simply wait it out until we eventually left. They knew it and we did too, but as long as the Marines had a mission in front of them, they would execute it without question. The bigger picture didn't matter to us when we were there. What mattered was going where our country felt it needed us to go and defending what we felt was right.

I left the cemetery with my mom and drove home. As soon as I got home, I got out of my desert camouflage uniform and changed into normal clothes and started drinking again. It was the only way I knew how to handle everything. If I was alone with my sober thoughts for even a moment, I knew I would collapse. I had just come from Afghanistan in the middle of my deployment to bury my friend and was set to return in a few days. I knew of no other way that I could enjoy myself without being too drunk to care about anything the entire time. At 21 years old, that's what I decided to do. I partied and drank like I was a college kid except with one major difference: I genuinely thought that there was a real chance that I would die in Afghanistan when I went back. I felt that the time at home may be the last I ever had and I was going to literally live like I was dying. I lived with recklessness and acted on impulse. I had parties at my mom's house, went out to the bars, and never stopped moving. I'm sure that everyone around me could see my alarming behavior but was probably too afraid to address it because they knew what I had been through and what I was going to go through in the near future. I'm sure many people felt that they'd be doing the same thing if they were in my situation. That behavior went on for a few days and then eventually slowed down, but I continued to drink heavily, just without the large parties. The people closest to me stayed around me the entire time I was home and I am forever grateful for them. That week at home for Nick's funeral was a blur. I had such a range of emotions and was totally exhausted, and on top of that I was drunk for the majority of it. I wish I could say that I conducted myself differently during that time, but I didn't have the tools I do now. I'm ashamed of how I acted during that time and carry it with me to this day. I felt like my emotional capacity reached its limit with the eulogy I spoke at Nick's funeral and the final burial of him. After those events, I had nothing left but the desire to drink until I could find some happiness in those moments with friends and family. I was also feeling an immense amount of guilt, shame, and sadness for leaving my Marines in Afghanistan. I needed to get back to Charlie Company as soon as possible.

BACK TO AFGHANISTAN

As my week at home was coming to an end, it started to dawn on me that I had no real idea of the process to get back into Afghanistan, then even further back to Charlie Company at the southernmost battle space of the entire Helmand Province. All I had was a ticket voucher that airlines would honor for any flight I needed. My mom dropped me off at Logan Airport in Boston and we had our emotional goodbyes. It was a difficult thing for me, but I'm sure it was far more difficult for her. I then got onto a flight that connected at the same airport in Portsmouth that I had arrived at a week earlier. From Portsmouth I got onto a flight that took me to Germany, then from Germany I flew back to Bagram Air Base. Each step of the way was confusing and difficult because I had no point of contact for any guidance. It felt like I was hitchhiking my way back into Afghanistan with the uncertainty of not knowing how long I'd be stuck at each step. Once at Bagram, I was finally able to meet up with a Marine liaison and told them my situation. That same day I got onto a helicopter that took me to Camp Leatherneck. The entire journey took around three days.

Once I got to Camp Leatherneck, I met with another Marine liaison who told me that my only option was to get on a supply convoy heading south because all of the helicopters were being used for a major battle that had just started in the Taliban stronghold city of Marjah.

Marjah was infamous to all Marines in Helmand. We'd been told that the invasion of it was being saved for after the rest of the Marine Expeditionary Brigade had secured the surrounding areas to isolate it. Once the battle began, the helicopters were needed for continual resupply and excavation of the wounded.

I was told that there was a convoy leaving the next morning that would eventually make its way to COP Payne where Charlie Company was located. This was great news because I wanted to get back there as soon as possible. The Marine directed me to a tent where Marines in supply and motor transport units were set up. He told me to sleep there and that he'd come to get me at 0500 am to leave on the convoy. The following morning I loaded up into the passenger seat of a seven-ton supply truck and we made our way out of the front gate of Camp Leatherneck. The convoy consisted of at least 20 vehicles and stretched a long distance as each vehicle kept space from the other in the event of an ambush. We had driven for approximately 20 minutes when I heard a loud explosion. I looked up and saw a big cloud of dust farther ahead in the convoy and realized that one of the vehicles had hit an IED. I was far away from the explosion so at the time it wasn't too alarming, and the occupants of the vehicle quickly reported that there were no casualties.

One of the vehicles had run over a small pressure plate, basically a home-made landmine, and it blew off one of its tires. Thankfully no one was hurt, but the entire convoy had to turn around and head back to Camp Leatherneck.

I assumed that the convoy would leave again the next morning, but that was not the case. I was told that future convoys would be heading to other parts of Helmand and it may be a few days until I could get on one again, that was around August 10th. I then went back to the tent I had slept in the night before and tried to get comfortable. I was extremely frustrated because I did not want to be stuck at Camp Leatherneck while my company and platoon were actively operating. The short break that Lt. Col. Grattan had assured me the company would take in my absence had come to an end and operations were back in full swing. Since Delta Company had secured the Khan Neshin Castle and the battle space around it, Charlie Company was operating out of COP Payne and pushing further south toward the Pakistan border. I spoke with a Marine who seemed to have a good knowledge of what was happening down there and he told me that while I was gone 3rd platoon, my platoon, had crossed the Helmand River and taken a serious amount of indirect fire from mortar rounds as they attempted to search a small village. During the mortar attack, one of the LAV-25s hit an IED and it completely disabled the vehicle. I asked if the Marine knew who was involved in the IED attack and he told me that the only name he knew was Gunnery Sergeant Washechecke and he was unsure of any injuries anyone in the vehicle sustained, but said that no one was killed.

I felt sick to my stomach after hearing that news. My worst fear had come true. My platoon had been in combat without me. I felt so ashamed for having gone home. What made things worse was that I still had no idea when I'd be getting back to my company. I had no purpose at Camp Leatherneck so every day was filled with anxiety and dread thinking about what I was missing while away from Charlie Company. I ate at the chow hall and read books all day in the tent trying to distract myself any way I could. I was stuck at Camp Leatherneck for around five days and it was absolutely miserable. Every day, I'd ask the motor transport Marines about the status of the convoy and each time was given no answer. Eventually I was told that one would be leaving early in the morning and to be prepared to get on it. I found the convoy and got in the passenger seat of a seven-ton truck just as I had before. We left in the same manner with approximately the same amount of vehicles and exited Camp Leatherneck.

This time, there was no IED strike and Camp Leatherneck disappeared behind us as we made our way deeper into Helmand Province through the endless flat desert.

The convoy moved slowly and had to stop regularly to check for suspected IEDs on the roads. The vehicles in the convoy did not have the same mobility and versatility as the LAV-25s so they had to stick to already established roads and routes. This was dangerous because those were the places most likely to have IEDs buried. It was a much different trip down south than I had done in July with Charlie Company. It was slow, hot, and painfully boring. Due to the fact that there were already established routes by then to travel south, the trip didn't take as long as the one in July. After a long day of travel, we made it to COP Payne and entered through the front guarded gate in the late afternoon as dusk was settling in. I could not believe that I was finally back there. In many ways, I felt more excited about returning to Charlie Company than I did when I went home. I felt that COP Payne was my home and I was back where I belonged. I jumped out of the vehicle and was excited to see that the entire company of LAV-25s was parked, which meant that they were not out on a mission. COP Payne had been considerably built up while I was gone and each platoon had its own large tent with cots in it. There were also makeshift showers that the engineers built by pumping the water from the Helmand River into a small rectangular building made from plywood with around six individual shower stalls. As I got closer to the tents, I saw Markusic and couldn't contain my excitement. I hugged him and told him I was glad to be back. I then met with my platoon commander, Lt. Mahoney. He told me how happy he was that I was back and asked me how things went back home with the funeral. I gave him the details and he said, "I'm glad you're back, we're heading out tomorrow morning for a mission across the river so get ready to get back in the saddle." I was happy to hear that because it would give me a chance to get right back into things and not dwell on the last two weeks. I needed my mind to be totally focused on what was in front of me. I then went to our tent and told all the other guys in my platoon about the funeral. None of them knew Nick but they all cared deeply about the situation and what it meant to me. After that I got comfortable and decided to write in my journal.

August 17th

For the first time in a long time I feel like I can breathe again and relax. I'm so happy to be back with my guys and to know everyone is alright. When I was sitting in Leatherneck I heard about Gunny Washechecke hitting that IED and I was really worried. Now that I'm back and know they're all fine I feel a lot better. Being here almost makes dealing with everything a lot easier.

None of these men knew Nick but yet that was the first thing all of them asked was how his family is and how the funeral went. I was worried everyone would be mad at me for going home but that wasn't the case at all and I'm relieved for that. I just miss Nick so much all the time it's painful.

When I sit and think about it too for too long I start crying and I feel like the world is caving in on me. There's so much more I wanted to say to Steve (Nick's father) when I was home but I just don't think I'd be able to hold up and feel like I'm the one who has to keep everyone else together. I felt like there was so much pressure on me, like everyone was looking to me for answers that I didn't have. I just don't feel right in my head anymore, almost like I'm lost and sometimes I think it's all a dream. It's like everything I do or think just reminds me of Nick and then I start crying again. I really do think that God is putting me through a test or trial to see how strong my character and will are and to see how I come out on the other end. I feel like these past and coming months are going to be what defines me as a man for the rest of my life and I really know in my heart that God and Nick are going to bring me home to everyone so I can start working on making sense of all this and help everyone else get through this. All I want is to be someone that people can look up to and be proud to have as a son, brother, or friend.

That night the company gathered for a briefing with all of the officers and vehicle commanders to go over the mission we'd be starting the next morning. I was eager and excited to get back out there. I needed so badly to get back in the swing of things and start operating at a fast pace again. I felt focused and driven in a way I hadn't in a long time. I felt that I needed to go out of my way to make up for my absence and the combat that I had missed. The briefing ended and I went to sleep. On August 18th at sunrise, we mounted our vehicles and departed through the rear gate of COP Payne to cross the Helmand River and head toward the Pakistan border for a four-day mission.

August 22nd

We just got back from a four day mission. We left for it the day after I got back here from being home. We left on a Wednesday I think and crossed the river to the same place that Gunny Washechecke hit his IED so we swept the whole route we were taking with metal detectors. Right by the first village they found two pressure plate IEDs so we all stopped and called up EOD (explosive ordinance disposal). It was near dusk at this point because the sweep took so long. My vehicle was about 100 yards away from the IED when EOD Gunny Benjamin walked up to it. I was just sitting on top of my vehicle looking at this compound with a lot of people in it when I saw the explosion go off. Gunny Benjamin was disarming the IED when it went off with him kneeling right next to it. I saw his body blow up into the air and then come crashing down nearby. We all had to pick up his body and put him into a body bag and then bring him back to COP Payne. Myself and Blue 4 brought him back and then just stayed at the edge of the river to watch for a mortar attack for the rest of the night. The next morning Blue 4 and I had to go back to COP Payne to pick up another EOD guy, Gunny Washechecke, and the remote controlled bomb detonator. Gunny went in my gunners seat, the robot in the back, and Cooke and Willie just squeezed in wherever they could. We crossed the river again and started back to the rest of the platoon. We got to a sand dune that we kept getting stuck on so I decided to go around and that's when the explosion happened. I ran over a buried IED and it hit my 3rd right tire, blowing up that whole side of the vehicle and throwing most of the stuff on top of it up in the air. My radios instantly went out so I started screaming asking who was hit. I couldn't my hear driver responding so I ripped open his hatch and pulled him out. He was very dazed but okay. Willie and Cooke said they were good and we started getting off of the vehicle. We came to find out that Willie had a grade 2 concussion. This is the most scared I've ever been in my entire life. I was shaking uncontrollably and threw up right when I got off and then just sat on the ground in a daze for a long time until my whole crew got MEDEVAC out by other vehicles. I have no doubt that in my mind that Nick was watching over us because if that had exploded under the 1st or 2nd tire, me and my driver would have been killed and everyone else seriously wounded. Death really is only just around the corner in this place and I can't wait to get out of here. I really do not want to see any more people die. I'm starting to see myself change from all this.

The events on August 18th and 19th were the lowest point of the deployment for me. I did not personally know Gunnery Sergeant Adam Benjamin because he had only been attached to our company for a short time, but the few interactions that I did have with him left an impression of a confident and seasoned Marine who loved his job of being an explosive ordnance disposal technician. I cannot imagine the courage it takes to put yourself in that amount of danger over and over again. The world of explosive ordinance disposal technicians is a small and elite community within the Marine Corps. They volunteer to walk straight up to unknown devices that are designed with the sole intention of killing a human by surprise. The devices are often booby-trapped or decoys used for a nearby secondary explosive device that is detonated when the technician is distracted by the decoy. The devices can also explode in the process of attempting to disarm them since they are homemade and the internal workings can be a mystery upon the first inspection. It is by far one of the most courageous, dangerous, and selfless jobs in the entire United States military. When an IED explodes, there is nothing glorious about it. More often than not, it happens out of nowhere and isn't connected to any sort of larger enemy engagement. There is no enemy to return fire against or seek retribution from. It is a terrifying and demoralizing reality of the situation that we were facing and once you experienced one IED blast, the psychological effect of driving or walking around wondering when the next one will strike is exhausting. I recall watching the Afghan people at the compound I had been monitoring observe the entire incident and they appeared completely unfazed by it. I'm sure they either planted the IED themselves, knew who planted it or did not care in the least that it had killed Gunny Benjamin. They continued about their business as though it was nothing more than an unwanted distraction interrupting their evening chores around their homes.

Adam Benjamin

The experience of hitting an IED is one I'll never forget. The one I ran over was buried in loose sand so while the explosion completely disabled my vehicle, it could have been a lot worse. If it had exploded toward the front of the vehicle instead of the middle, it would most likely have killed my driver, Jake Tyrell, and either killed or seriously wounded me. When the explosion happened, everything went dark because of the sand and dust blown up into the air. I felt the force of the explosion ripple through my insides and lift my feet off the floor as my hearing turned into a loud ringing sound. Once I realized that I was not hurt, my immediate thoughts went to Tyrell in the driver's compartment. I envisioned opening the hatch and seeing him dead inside as a mangled mess of body parts. The driver's compartment is such a small and enclosed space that if an explosion went off underneath it, there would be no chance of survival, as we had sadly already learned with the IED Master Sergeant Hatfield and Lance Corporal Barboza-Flores hit. Once I pulled him out and realized he was uninjured, I started worrying about the rest of the crew, but I heard them talking in the back of the LAV saying that they were uninjured. We all eventually got out of the vehicle and sat down nearby but there was still the threat of secondary IEDs so we had to sweep the area with a metal detector. It was obvious to me that Willie was far more dazed and out of it than the rest of the crew. He said that when the explosion went off, one of the stacked TOW missiles came loose and landed directly on his head. My crew, Gunny Washechecke, and I were all transported back to COP Payne by vehicles sent out to get us. Once back we all went to the aide station to get checked out. Willie clearly had a bad concussion but Cooke and Tyrell did not look good either. I could tell they were both dazed and shaken up. All three of them were inside the vehicle when the explosion happened while I had my upper body exposed outside of the vehicle commander's hatch. The explosion was extremely loud for me but I did not suffer the same concussive effects of the blast as everyone inside. To add to the already bad situation, the vehicle that we had been living out of since July was destroyed and I was not happy about it. That LAV-AT meant a lot to us and we had customized it for ourselves so it felt like home. I was worried that I would be displaced without a vehicle and stuck inside COP Payne while the rest of the platoon and company continued operating.

As soon as I got done checking in at the aide station, Gunny Washechecke asked me if I wanted to go back out and take command of another LAV-AT to continue with the mission. The last thing I wanted to do was sit on COP Payne while the rest of the platoon carried on, so I said yes and we were both transported back to our platoon across the river. Willie, Tyrell and Cooke stayed on COP Payne to be monitored for any serious effects of the concussions they had. I'm sure none of them wanted to stay behind either, but it was the right thing for them to do at the time. I took over as the vehicle commander of the LAV-AT which my good friend Markusic was a gunner on. We continued with the mission and returned to COP Payne on August 21st.

Once that mission was over, I became concerned about getting another LAV-AT for my crew and me as quickly as possible. I asked Lt. Mahoney what the plan was and he told me that my crew and I would be going back to Camp Leatherneck with a supply convoy to pick up another LAV-AT and drive it back to COP Payne with the convoy. I was thrilled with this idea because it would give my crew a chance to go to Leatherneck and eat real food and take real showers for the first time in over a month and we'd be getting a new vehicle. The trip to Leatherneck went quickly and smoothly. At that point, the route was being used so frequently that it was a straight shot with no need to stop along the way. We got to Leatherneck and immediately went to the chow hall. At the time we were wearing what is called FROG (**F**ire **R**etardant **O**uter **G**arment) suits, which are Marine desert camouflage uniforms but much lighter and the top is basically a long sleeve tee shirt with only the exposed camouflaged sleeves that stick out from the plate carrier. Apparently, this dirty uniform did not meet the standard of what was allowed to be worn inside the chow hall on Camp Leatherneck. A Staff Sergeant stopped us at the entrance and told us that unless we had traditional Marine desert camouflage uniforms on, we could not go in.

I looked at the Marine in disbelief and almost laughed at how ridiculous his statement was. I explained that we just came from the southernmost battle area of the entire operation and these were the only uniforms we had and the only uniforms our entire company was wearing. I explained all of this to him respectfully because I knew arguing with someone of that rank and that mindset would not end well for me. What I thought to myself however was that we were not sitting on a massive base insulated from the reality of what was happening in Helmand Province and this guy should get the fuck out of our way and let us eat. This situation was a good example of some of the friction that occurs in the Marine Corps and the divide that happens between the infantry along with their supporting forward operating units and the other specialty jobs. When the U.S. spends as much time as they did in a place like Afghanistan, they build huge military bases. The longer they are there the more the bases get built up to provide the comforts of America. Many Marines and Sailors deploy to these bases and are confined to them for the entire deployment because their specialty job requires them to be there. It is not their fault, and I'm sure that many of them wish they were with the forward operating units, but it creates a divide between the people living in dangerous and rugged conditions and the people living in safety and comforts of established military bases. The Staff Sergeant must have felt bad because he eventually let us in and we stuffed our faces then left. We were then directed to our new vehicle and tested everything out. We stayed overnight at Leatherneck then left the next morning to head back to COP Payne with no issues along the way.

Toward the end of August, engineers came down to start building a forward outpost on the southern side of the Helmand River in order to establish a permanent foothold in the area we continually ran into trouble when patrolling. Once the outpost was built, we could continue to make our way closer to the Pakistan border without having to return to COP Payne each time. It was decided that my platoon would live at the outpost along with a platoon of Afghan National Army soldiers (ANA). We were to assist in training the ANA while continuing to patrol the surrounding area.

The process of building the outpost took quite a while and involved the entire platoon posted up in a security circle with our vehicles while the engineers used bulldozers and other equipment to build it. It was an extremely boring time for us and the days were long and uneventful. I recall only one day during the building of the outpost that we came under mortar fire and it consisted of only one round landing far enough away from my vehicle that I wasn't overly concerned with it. The Marines at COP Payne got an idea of where it was coming from and returned their own mortar fire.

The outpost was named South Station and was a large rectangle that consisted of a controlled entry point with a guarded gate and four additional guard towers that faced in each direction. The walls were made of Hesco barriers. A Hesco barrier is a combination of a welded wire mesh frame on the outside with a woven cloth liner on the inside that is shaped in a large square and filled with sand. They are approximately seven feet tall by seven feet wide and can withstand small arms fire and rocket attacks. They were stacked two on top of each other and constructed into a square perimeter that formed the body of the outpost. The inside of the outpost had three large tents for us, a tent for the ANA platoon, a tent for a command post with all of our communication equipment inside, and a large gas-powered generator. We also had a makeshift chow hall area with an overhang and tables. Once it was fully built and we were set up inside, it became somewhat comfortable. It was also nice to be out on our own and away from the rest of the company for a change. During this phase of the deployment, there was a lot of down-time and I began to think way too much. I began to get very down on myself and also directed my anger about Nick's death toward some of the people back home. At the time, I began to feel that many of those people didn't actually care about what was going on in Afghanistan until Nick was killed. I convinced myself that many were seeking their own attention through Nick's death while also feeling incredibly ashamed and guilty for the attention that I was getting as a result of it. This was a trend that would continue for the rest of the deployment and is continually brought up in my journal entries. These things were not entirely true, but those were the thoughts of my 21-year-old mind at the time. With that much guilt, shame, and anger being internally dealt with, it only made sense that I directed it somewhere other than the Marines around me who I cared so deeply about.

COP South Station

September 4th

Well it's September now and our platoon has moved south across the river to build a road and an outpost south of the river. We've been sitting out here posting up security for the engineers for the last 5 or 6 days and besides one mortar round hitting about 300 meters off from us nothing has happened. It seems to be getting a little cooler during the day and actually cold at night. Last night we found out that Doc Peterson and another corpsman were killed by a pressure plate that was setup right inside the doorway of a house they were walking into. Three other Marines were wounded from the blast but I'm not sure how badly or who they were.

That brings our casualty number to six KIA and I think five wounded. I knew Doc Peterson pretty well, he was a really nice guy and was always friendly to me and made sure to say hi whenever he saw me. I feel like now I just put that kind of stuff in the back of my head because it just brings up memories and reminds me of everything and then I start to lose focus. It seems like whenever it's quiet here for too long it always builds up to something very bad like that happening. Every time I start to get miserable or frustrated I just think about how happy and grateful I am to be alive no matter what I'm doing that day. All of this support from back home is great I guess but I have mixed feelings about it. It seems to like a lot of people are trying to replace Nick with me in their minds and are making me out to be some kind of hero and I can't stand it. Just the fact that there was only about three people who sent me mail before and now the whole damn class of 2006 does says something. Where were all these people when I broke my hips? Or where were they when Nick and I got back from Iraq? I guess that's just the way people are though. People don't understand the way Marines die off here either. You can do nothing and be bored out of your mind for two or three days then on that fourth day you're driving or walking and just get blown to pieces by an IED. There's nothing glorious about it, you don't die in the midst of some heroic act, you're just dead and your body along with the wounded get MEDVAC out and the mission continues on. Not to say that everyone isn't traumatized by it, but what can you really do? Charlie Company, especially our platoon, has had some outstanding luck out here and I think we are all walking on eggshells now just waiting to go back home. I think going back home now too is going to be a lot harder than being out here is. At least everyone out here knows how this shit works.

Mid September

We have built the south station base across the river and have now pulled the whole platoon into it. It's actually pretty nice here, there's a lot of work to be done but at least the company leaves us alone. It has started to cool down too and at night and in the morning it's actually really cold and feels very good. I guess Doc Peterson wasn't killed by that IED he was just wounded badly to the head and face but is still alive. The two that did die are names I remember but can't put faces with them, but I'm sure I knew them. I feel like the closer we get to going back home the less excited I feel about it. There's just a lot of things I'm going to have to face now and I'm nervous about everything. How is Nick's family going to handle me celebrating to be back home without Nick? I don't know I'm going to handle it. Nothing feels right anymore and I think it's going to get a lot worse before it gets better. Nick was the only one that knew what this was like and now I'm all alone and everyone else like John and Josh (close friends from back home and also Marines in different units) want to come here and think they're going to be bad ass or something. I can't really blame them though, me and Nick were like that before we came here. In some ways I feel numb to the whole thing, I can't remember the last time I cried about it and even if I want to most times I feel like I can't. Everyone out here has lost something so it's hard to really bring it up to anyone.

The IED blast mentioned in these two journal entries involved Delta Company, which at that time was still operating in the battle space of the Khan Neshin Castle. Charlie Company had little involvement with Delta and we often heard second or third-hand information on what was happening with them, which is why I heard misinformation about Corpsman Peterson being killed. The Marine Corps doesn't have medics like the army, Navy Hospital Corpsman serve as medics and are attached to infantry platoons and are referred to as "Doc." I was not present for the incident, but what I do know is that an IED blast occurred on September 3rd, 2009, that killed 21-year-old Navy Corpsman Petty Officer 3rd Class Benjamin Castiglione, and 19-year-old Lance Corporal Christopher Baltazar Jr. A 20-year-old Lance Corporal Christopher Fowlkes was severely wounded by the blast and died in a military hospital in Germany on September 10th 2009. I had met all of them at one point but did not personally know any of these men. I still felt a deep sadness for their loss. All I could picture in my mind was what their families and loved ones were going through back home. All of these men had their own stories and were heroes to their families and communities.

Benjamin Castiglione   *Christopher Baltazar Jr.*   *Christopher Fowlkes*

Once we were fully set up in the south station outpost, life settled into a bit of a routine compared to the previous months. I have no idea how, but we were somehow able to get a volleyball for our platoon. We began to have fun and play makeshift volleyball games and work out doing bodyweight circuits. Once in a while the ANA soldiers would get in on the volleyball games, but since the only sport they had ever seen or played was soccer, they'd end up just kicking the ball around. We still went on missions on a regular basis to patrol closer to the Pakistan border, but they were more regularly scheduled and our operation tempo began to slow down. Everyone felt that we were getting close to the end despite the fact that we had two full months left. I wouldn't say that we were getting complacent, but we were certainly getting used to being there by then. We were also getting mail on a regular basis which made a huge difference for our morale. Instead of eating nothing but MREs, we began snacking on whatever was sent to us from back home. My biggest request was Marlboro light cigarettes, Monster Energy drinks, and ramen noodles. We'd all barter and trade amongst ourselves when the care packages arrived. With all of the new comforts came a lot of time for me to think, and that was the last thing I needed at that time. I began to get angry and depressed but internalized it and did not show it on the outside. Instead of being thankful for the overwhelming support from back home, I continued to direct my anger toward people back home who I felt had never cared to begin with. In hindsight I know that's not true, people only wanted to help in any way they could, but in my mind I felt bitter about it at the time. I also began to blame myself for Nick coming to Afghanistan at all. I felt that he had volunteered for the transfer to 2/8 in large part because I had talked up the upcoming deployment so much. In my heart I knew that wasn't the truth. Nick would have gone regardless of anything I did or said, but I just felt so angry and the only place I could direct that anger was at myself and some of the people back home. A large part of my anger was also directed at myself for going home in the middle of the deployment and leaving my Marines. I carried a lot of guilt and shame over that decision.

September 22

It feels like we are close to leaving but we really aren't. There's still a lot that can happen in the time we have left. Not much has been going on for our platoon, there has been shit going on though. Mortars are shot pretty much regularly, Recon (Marine Recon unit operating with us) took a wounded casualty then called in a 500 pound bomb on the target a couple miles from here. There was a big raid that went down a couple of nights ago too. I really am ready to get out of here, it just feels like time is dragging by and it's still hot as hell out. I just feel annoyed all the time by everything like I'm going to snap. I find that every day I have to find a reason to be happy, just to be alive is a good enough one. There's not a minute of the day that goes by that I don't think about Nick. I don't get why I'm alive and he's not, it just doesn't make sense to me. I guess it's all part of a plan. It makes me wonder what I'm being kept around for. It's a very difficult feeling to live with and as we get closer to leaving it feels worse. I don't even know if I'm going to go away to college now, I can't do it alone and I don't want to do it with anyone but Nick. I think the fire academy is a good idea, that would get me right into something without giving me time to fuck anything up when I get out. It also seems like a career I would really like and I could also start my own business at the same time. I just need to maintain focus in these months after I get out. I get excited thinking about it sometimes then I think about all these things Nick and I should have both been doing and I feel guilty in a way. All this may pass for a lot of people but this summer of 2009 will never pass for me or Nick's family, nothing is ever going to be the same again. I find myself just angry all the time too. I'm angry about all these people who probably didn't even know we were in Afghanistan and are now acting like they know me so well. I just can't live with the feeling of me benefiting from my friend dying and I feel like that's exactly what is happening. I just feel like no one has gotten or helped me to where I am but me and I don't need anyone's help now. I guess I could go on all day about this but I really have nothing else to do or think about it. I just feel so messed up in my head all the time like I'm going crazy or something. Another thing that's been really bothering me is that I know for a fact that Nick wouldn't have come here if I didn't. Maybe if I hadn't even talked it all up like I did he wouldn't have come and he would be sitting on Lejeune waiting for me when I got off the bus with a cooler full of beer. I guess it doesn't do any good to think like that though.

I am really excited about seeing Tibbetts (John Tibbetts, a close friend from home and Marine stationed at Lejeune). I feel like it's been a year since I have. Maybe he'll want to go to the fire academy too.

As we continued to live alongside and train the Afghan National Army soldiers, it became very obvious to us that there was no chance they would ever be able to handle operating on their own. The platoon commander appeared to have military bearing and discipline, but the rest of them did not seem to care at all. The idea of Afghanistan standing on its own as a democratic nation with its own army and police force seemed so clearly ridiculous to me then that I wondered how any reasonable politician could look at the situation and even think it was a possibility. They did nothing all day long and never left the outpost to do patrols of their own. I had no confidence in their ability to fight alongside us if need be and I did not trust them. For all we knew they were either former or current Taliban members. We kept them at a cautious distance but tolerated them as much as we needed to. They were not all bad people, just not soldiers and victims of the realities of being born in a place like Afghanistan. Some tried their best to interact with us and wanted to do their part for their country, but the ones who didn't care made their unit look so bad that it didn't matter. They also became very needy as time went on and requested to take trips to the nearest bazaar, a Middle Eastern term for marketplace. It was a good distance away and they couldn't do it on their own because they drove in only seven-ton troop carrier vehicles with no real security. On October 4th, they requested to go and half the platoon was tasked with taking them while the rest stayed behind at the outpost.

October 4th

Today Blue 3 and Blue 4 went out to bring the ANA to the market in Pay Banada, going past the high ground we always use. Blue 3 hit an IED and my vehicle and Blue 1 left to go to them with me leaving first. We got there and I got out to help with the three casualties and saw that Lcpl. Wege had both of his feet blown to pieces, one was completely gone and the other was crushed so bad it was going to get cut off anyway. We all started helping to get them out of there. My two good friends Cpl. Mathis and Lcpl. Howard were both injured. Mathis had a ruptured spleen and lots of internal bleeding while Howard had small shrapnel wounds. It's the fourth IED we've hit and this was the worst of all of them. I really want to go home. It seems that every time you get comfortable something like this happens. I just feel old and tired, like I've been drained of everything. There's not a minute of the day I don't think about Nick or if something is going to happen to me this last month. At least it is still getting cooler out and I am still alive.

That IED blast occurred on a dirt road essentially in the middle of nowhere. It was a clear, sunny, and uneventful day that turned into chaos simply because the ANA wanted to go to the bazaar to get food. There was no mission taking place, no enemy being pursued, and certainly no ability to retaliate. For all we knew, that IED had been buried for weeks and we just happened to drive down that road on that particular day. The total randomness of it was far more terrifying than being engaged by a clear enemy who we could fight back against. L.Cpl. Joshua Wege ultimately got both of his feet amputated from the injuries he suffered. He was 19 years old at the time and would spend the rest of his life as a double amputee from the knees down.

October 5th

I haven't written anything in here for a while prior to yesterday and after what happened I just feel like writing down what's been going through my head. I feel like I've fallen into some sort of depression these last two weeks or so. Nick being gone has hit me harder than it ever has. I find myself angry all the time. I'm angry about people now caring all of a sudden about me and Nick doing all of this. I feel like for a lot of people it's just a reason to get together and party. Or it's a way for them to bullshit everyone on how close they were with Nick, and now in turn they're doing the same to me. Lately I've been really thinking about how Nick and Q wouldn't have even come here if it weren't for me. I think about how I don't know why Nick died and I lived. Nick was ten times the man, Marine, and person I could ever be. He was the only one who kept me from doing the stupid shit I would do and really caused me to be the way I am now. I don't think anyone knew him like I did. I'm afraid of what's going to happen to me without him around now, I just feel so alone when everyone is around me. I don't even really want to go to college anymore because we were supposed to do it together . I think about when I go home and everyone is celebrating and it's going to be all happening again for Nick's family because he won't be home too this time. I don't even know if Q is still alive either and I think about that every day too. We were all just as much a part of this as the other. That's one thing I guarantee all these people back home don't know. How the three of us came here together, and now maybe only one if any of us is going to be walking out of this. I feel like what's happened this summer is just a slight speed bump in most people's care free college lives. I feel like these people are just kids while I feel old and jaded and worn out. I've experienced and seen things out here that would cause any one of my friends and even older people back home to buckle at their knees and curl up into a ball and probably start crying. I can't explain the way things go with this stuff to anyone and I don't really care about doing it either. I just really miss my friend so much that I feel like crying all day sometimes. I have to try to keep it in the back of my head though, because as yesterday showed, we are not done or out of here yet.

I was so sad and angry about Nick dying that it started consuming me. I didn't want to be in Afghanistan, but didn't want to go home either. I was simply a kid who lost his friend and didn't know how to deal with it at that age. At that point in my life I hadn't dealt with loss enough to have the tools to make sense of it. It was overwhelming me and I increasingly continued to place blame on myself while also directing anger at people back home who only had good intentions. The more downtime we had the worse these feelings got for me. None of these emotions ever carried over to the Marines around me and I dealt with them all internally or wrote in my journal. I started to feel that every time I wrote in my journal I was complaining, and that made me even more angry at myself. It was a vicious cycle and the downtime during the deployment caused that cycle to continue on and on. In hindsight I believe that going home for Nick's funeral and the emotional drain that it put on me made me dwell on his death much more than I would have if I had stayed in Afghanistan and continued operating. Having seen first-hand the pain everyone was going through back home made it much more real than if I had stayed in Afghanistan. I also began to dwell on the fact that I'd be getting discharged from the Marine Corps seven months after we got back and the thought of losing that structure in my life was starting to scare me the closer it got.

October 24th

The closer we get to going home the less excited about it I am. It just feels hard to get excited about anything without Nick. I miss him so much I don't feel good or normal now. Everything reminds me of him. It's just hard to imagine what I'm going to do now especially when I'm getting out when we get back. This is probably the biggest crossroad in life I'll ever face. I go to sleep every night hoping he'll come in a dream and tell me what to do. I'm thinking I might just go away for a while and clear my head by myself. We have one more operation coming up on the 28th and then that's it. I really hope nothing happens on it so we can all go home. I'm not worried about anything happening to me anymore. If it does it does and I'll be able to see Nick so at least I can take comfort in that much. I just wish people would realize how insignificant life's little problems are and enjoy it. It really just amazes me the things some people will never know. I don't think any of the people I know back home know what it's like to be truly miserable or just drained of everything. I just miss my friend is all and it's going to be really hard to do these things we all had planned by myself.

We were all excited about the upcoming mission on October 28th. It was the first mission the entire company was coordinating together in quite some time and preparing for it was exciting. Since I was a vehicle commander, I was in the briefings with the officers and saw how the plans were made behind the scenes. Our mission was to travel about 40 kilometers north to the Taliban stronghold of Safar Bazaar. It was part of the Garmsir district, the same area where Nick had been killed, and was the center of the opium trade. It was reported that the bazaar was full of civilians and Taliban that would need to be cleared out. Once the bazaar was secured, we were to look for any opium stashes and destroy them before the upcoming harvest season. Commanders thought that disrupting the opium harvest and trade would severely impact the Taliban's ability to conduct operations as it was their primary source of income. The problem with that idea was that while it was the Taliban's main source of income, it was also the only source of income for the local population. They had no other goods to produce or sell to make a living. Depriving the civilian population of their opium production and trade was an extremely unpopular move against a people that we were trying to win over and establish a relationship with. While the civilians lived in fear of the Taliban and their oppressive rule, they also understood that they could live prosperous lives with the security they provided. The vast majority of people in the Helmand Province sided with the Taliban and wanted foreigners out of their lands.

We had previously been to the Safar Bazaar in early July when we were still establishing our area of operations but found no opposition there, as all of the Taliban were busy fighting with 2/8 in the center of Garmsir. We found several tons of the poppy seed that is used to make opium and gathered it all in a huge pile to destroy it. We realized that we could not light the pile on fire ourselves, so we called in for air support to drop a bomb on it. An F-18 fighter jet dropped a bomb on the pile and it exploded into flames and destroyed the seeds. We knew that this greatly upset the Taliban and civilians so we were expecting resistance the second time going there.

Charlie Company left at dusk on October 28th in a long column of vehicles organized into each platoon. Once we got to the high ground of the open desert, we set up in a security circle and waited for darkness to continue the movement. The movement was done in total blackout conditions and it was an extremely dark night with no moonlight. Our only way to see was with night vision goggles that could be nauseating to look through for extended periods of time. The only people who actually needed to see were the vehicle commanders and the drivers. I could at least take the goggles off every so often, but the drivers had to look at their night vision screens the entire time. It is a very difficult way to drive a large armored vehicle because there is no depth perception and you can't tell where soft sand or ditches are. Once we started the journey we did not stop for any reason. If a vehicle got stuck or had a mechanical issue, it was their problem to solve and catch up with the company. We also could not allow any vehicles to approach the convoy in fear that they may be hostile or even suicide bombers. If any vehicle approached, we would fire warning shots, and if it continued to approach, we would open fire on it. This occurred one time during the movement and 1st platoon opened fire on an approaching vehicle with its 25-millimeter cannon. The vehicle stopped dead in its tracks and we continued with no further issues.

We arrived at the Safar Bazaar on the morning of October 29th and established a perimeter around it. The bazaar consisted of mud buildings and narrow roads that connected in a grid-like pattern. All of the buildings were one story high and many had approximately six-foot-high walls around them. There were also open market areas with stands set up for the sale of produce and other goods. Once we established our perimeter, our Afghan interpreters began announcing over loudspeakers that anyone left in the bazaar should come out peacefully or they may be considered hostile. The announcements had no effect. The scouts and EOD technician Marines then dismounted the vehicles and began making their way into the bazaar. There were IEDs immediately found all over the roads. Within the first hour, there were 10 located and the EOD Marines began doing controlled detonations of them. The explosions went on for hours and the movement inside the bazaar was slow and methodical. The Taliban must have known we were coming because the bazaar which was normally busy with activity and rumored to have around 800 people in it, was empty except for a few suspicious locals who decided to stay and were most likely lookouts for the Taliban nearby watching us. My vehicle was positioned about 100 yards outside of the bazaar while over watching the scouts as they discovered the IEDs and pushed deeper into the town. It is a miracle that no one was wounded or killed in that bazaar.

There were so many IEDs buried and waiting for us that all day long, there was explosion after explosion. The EOD technicians had a long and dangerous day of finding those IEDs and detonating them while the infantry scouts cleared the surrounding areas and kept watch on security while every step they took could land on an IED that was missed.

Around noon time we began taking 107 mm rocket fire from a nearby hill. Two rounds landed between my vehicle and 1st platoon located a short distance away from me. We were able to locate where the fire was coming from and could see a group of four men setting up to fire rockets at us from a compound. 1st platoon engaged the four men with their 25-millimeter cannons and killed all four. We could see more men gathering in the area so we called in artillery to take out the entire compound. A short time later, the artillery rounds came soaring overhead and landed approximately 500 yards off of the target. Our own mortars decided it would be easier to handle the problem themselves and fired rounds into the compound until it was destroyed while 1st platoon continued to fire their 25-millimeter high explosive rounds. It was exciting to watch and wildly disproportionate to the fire we were receiving but we felt no remorse unloading on the compound knowing that the occupants of it had buried all those IEDs in hopes of killing us. There was no chance anyone in or near that compound was still alive.

They had made a huge mistake by firing those rockets at us and paid dearly for it.

One thing that is not often talked about is how excited Marines are to use their weapons in combat. Marines train for months with their weapons systems and fire thousands of rounds at inanimate targets while hoping for the chance to test their skills during combat. When contact with the enemy starts, the mostly 19-23-year-old-testosterone-filled Marines are beyond excited to return fire. This creates a response that can be almost comically disproportional to the threat. No Marine wants to come back from a combat deployment having not fired their weapon, so they take any chance they get to do so. It is a large part of what makes the Marine Corps so effective. Marines are all kept pissed off and over trained so that they are dying at the chance to take it out on the enemy.

We stayed at the bazaar and continued to search it until October 31st then made the journey back south. My platoon went back to our south station outpost while the rest of Charlie Company went to COP Payne. The uneventful movement was done at night and we arrived at South Station outpost on the morning of November 1st. When we got back, we were excited to find that mail had been delivered while we were gone. My 22nd birthday was on October 31st so it was an especially welcomed surprise for me. In one of the packages, I found three nips of Jack Daniels whiskey that my lifelong friend from home, Brendan Walker, had hidden within other items. I waited until night time then mixed the three nips with a Monster Energy drink, sat on top of a Hesco barrier and drank them while looking up at the stars, listening to my iPod to celebrate my 22nd birthday. The night sky in Afghanistan is one of the most beautiful sights I've ever seen. The high elevation and lack of unnatural light pollution allow you to see the Milky Way and more stars than I could have ever imagined. It looked as though you could jump off the ground and fall into the universe. I was happy in that moment.

Overwatch at Safar Bazaar

November 2nd

So we went up to Safar Bazaar again on the 28th for a three day operation with all of Charlie Company. We pulled up to the town on the morning of the 29th and all of the scouts along with the Afghan Army began to push into the bazaar after announcing over the loudspeakers for all of the civilians to come out. The loudspeaker had no effect so they just pushed in anyway. My vehicle along with the rest of 3rd platoon was staged about 100 meters outside of the city over-watching the scouts movement. As soon as they entered the bazaar area the first IED was found and it had multiple wires running off of it in different directions. The EOD tech set charges on the first IED and blew it in place causing a very large explosion. IED's continued to be found like this all day and were blown in place by our EOD tech to eliminate them. All together I think there were 10 IED's found on the first road leading into the bazaar area. At about noon 107 mm rockets started getting shot at us that kept landing between myself and 1st platoon's position on a hill to the right of where I was parked. Two landed within about an hour pretty accurately in the area before we discovered where they were coming from inside the city. 1st platoon's Red 1 vehicle saw the people in a group of four setting up to shoot another rocket about 1200 meters to the northeast of him and engaged with 25 mm high explosive rounds to keep them from firing the rocket. They realized that there were more people in the tree line and compound where this came from so artillery was called in to take out the whole area. I had a very clear view of all this where my vehicle was. I heard the artillery shells soaring over my head and saw them impact about 500 meters off to the right of the target in the complete wrong compound. To correct this problem instead of having the artillery adjust their fire we decided to use our own mortar team. The mortars did an immediate suppression of 10 rounds and landed right on target. While this was going on 1st platoon was still firing 25 mm high explosive rounds the entire time. This went on for probably more than an hour and continued almost until dark. It was definitely a little extreme for the situation to use that much fire power but it was very entertaining to watch and you really don't care when these people either planted or knew about those 10 IED's waiting for us. Nobody with us got hurt through all of this either so that made it even more enjoyable. When we got back we had mail waiting for us. Most of the letters and packages were sent for my birthday so it was nice. I got a box from Brendan (a close friend from back home) that had three nips of Jack Daniels in it so I was very excited about that. Everyone seems excited that it's November now and it's only a matter of a few weeks until we go home. Sometimes I am excited I guess but most of the time I'm not. I just feel like there's not much to be excited about anymore no matter how hard I try. I feel very unsure of whether I should get out or not now too. I wish I knew what John Tibbetts was planning on doing I think would help a lot in making up my mind.

After the operation at the Safar Bazaar, the entire company transitioned into a defensive role as we maintained our positions and awaited 4th Light Armored Reconnaissance Battalion to arrive and relieve us and Delta Company. We weren't hiding inside the walls of our outposts, but we had no offensive missions planned. It was also starting to get a lot colder out, which historically caused the Taliban to slow down their operations as well. 4th LAR arrived in early November and we began our RIP (**R**elief **I**n **P**lace), which consisted of their Marines mirroring us on patrols to get an idea of the battle space and problem areas they'd be facing. Much of the RIP focused on our officers going on patrols with the new officers replacing them to show them the methods and tactics that we'd adopted over the last seven months. Once the Marines of 4th LAR felt that they had a good enough grasp on the situation, we ceased all of our own patrols and gave them our vehicles and equipment. At that point, my platoon relocated back to COP Payne with the rest of Charlie Company. We then began the process of inventorying our gear and preparing for the movement back to Camp Leatherneck to start our journey home.

November 16th

We are getting closer and closer to going home now. From what I've been told Q is already home which I'm really happy about. I think we are getting back on the 26th which is Thanksgiving day. That is not good because that means no one will be at the battalion and a lot of stuff will be closed. As of right now it doesn't seem like anyone is going to be able to come down for the homecoming. It would be so expensive that it almost seems like it wouldn't be worth it. I really want to see Q right away when I get back but he'll probably be home for the holidays. So will all of my friends that didn't deploy so I'm not sure how I'm going to get anywhere. I guess you could say I'm really not that excited to get back. I had a very strange dream a few nights ago that I can't get out of my head. I can't really remember it that clearly but I do remember most of it. I was in some house from my childhood, I'm not sure where exactly, but I was on the phone in a living room talking to Nick as I am in the present. I said, "Nick, how am I talking to you? You're dead.". He just started laughing and said, "Don't worry about all that.". I asked, "What's it like there?", and he said "It's great I love it.". I told him how everyone is a mess over him and how much I wish I could just go to where he was and get away from all this. He said, "Don't worry you'll be here someday.". I asked when and he told me to stop worrying so much. I asked if I could ever call him back on the phone and he said no. I woke up after that all confused in the tent here on COP Payne and wanted to go back to sleep so I could continue the dream, but I couldn't sleep anymore. It was the first time since Nick died that I've had a dream involving him and it just left me feeling really unsettled. I really thought that out of Nick, Q, and myself that if anyone was going to die out here it would have been me. The unexplained guilt that I feel every minute of every hour of every day for it not being me is just too much sometimes. I hope that when I can talk to Q maybe we can both find some peace because I know he has to be suffering just as badly and he hasn't had anyone to go to. Him not going to the funeral while I did is another thing I feel constant guilt over.

That was the last entry I ever made in that journal. After November 16th, we began our journey home by leaving COP Payne in helicopters for Camp Leatherneck. Once at Leatherneck, we were set up in the same style tents we had lived in back in May and waited for our next leg of the journey home to begin. We all ate at the chow hall, took showers, and used the phone centers to call home and update our families. You could feel the sense of relief everyone had for being in the safety of Camp Leatherneck, knowing that we were heading home. It was a strange feeling for me because I had already been home once during the deployment but under such drastically different circumstances. I had mixed emotions about going home again but still felt excited to be leaving Afghanistan and going back to the comforts of America. I also found out that my mom would be there for my return and that she planned on renting a condo in Topsail Island, North Carolina for a few days so we could be away from Camp Lejeune. Those few days went by fast at Camp Leatherneck as we all acclimated to the improved surroundings and the excitement of going home.

One morning we were told by our company commander, Captain Connor, that the commanding General of the entire MEB, Brigadier General Nicholson, wanted to speak with us before we left. We all gathered outside of our tents on a cool sunny morning in a circle around the General. Brigadier General Nicholson had the command presence and look of a warfighter. He had a rough and grizzled appearance with a booming voice that commanded attention. We all stood at attention, waiting for him to speak when he smiled and said, "At ease gentlemen." He began by saying, "There's no one who did more with less for this mission than all of you, you were under-equipped, under-supplied, and had the least support of any part of this MEB, I am proud of you all." The statement was not intended to take away from all the other Marines and Sailors who took part in Operation Khanjar but he was simply saying that because we were the furthest from the supply routes, had the largest battle space, and the smallest amount of Marines and Sailors, that we had exceeded all his expectations. I have no doubt that Brigadier General Nicholson addressed all the battalions involved in the operation and gave them their well-deserved recognition, but to hear it directly from the man meant a lot in that moment. It made me feel like we had been part of history, part of something special, something that would be remembered for years to come. It was a moment that would stick with me for the rest of my life.

GOING HOME

It's difficult to describe the feeling of going home after a deployment. It's a moment you wait so long for, and endure so much to get to, that by the time it arrives, it almost seems surreal. You begin to think about what happened on the deployment in a third-person perspective, trying to make sense of events that you took part in but can't rationalize, so the only way you can picture it is through the lens of someone else watching. You also get overwhelmed with the reality of finally reaching a moment you've waited so long for. You start to wonder what you'll actually do once you're back and how things will feel. I had all of these thoughts but mixed with the confusion of having already gone home once, but for a reason that brought me no happiness. It made me feel the final journey home could only be anticlimactic and filled with the guilt of returning when Nick and many others were not. I pushed those thoughts into the back of my mind and tried my best to replace them with excitement to see my mom and friends. I knew that my coming home would be a massive burden lifted off of my mom's shoulders. I felt that she endured far more than I did over those seven months.

We landed at Cherry Point Air Base in North Carolina in the late afternoon on November 26th as planned. As the plane landed, the pilot came over the loudspeaker and said, "Welcome back to the United States of America." The feeling of hearing those words filled me with so much pride and joy that it brought me to tears. The high of emotions you get from coming home from a combat deployment are hard to compare to anything else in life. I feel that I've never let go of that high and much of my life now consists of chasing it. I live in the highest of highs or lowest of lows and I have a very difficult time living in the middle. I have found this to be common among all of my friends who deployed and saw combat. It's as though you never really come down from that high of emotions; you just try to replace them as time goes on and fail more often than not. The transition back to what's considered to be "normal" life is a difficult one and the masculinity, pride, and ego attached to being a Marine forces many Marines, including me, to figure that transition out on their own. The idea of seeking help is a difficult thing to do at that time in your life but in reality, it's the only way to move forward. Everyone gets help from someone, and the sooner we all realize that and take the help that is offered, the sooner we can be in a position to help someone else going through the same things. It took me many years to overcome my own stubbornness and realize that. Even now at 36 years old, I often find myself in a waking daydream, thinking about these things that mean nothing in the grand scheme of things but everything to me. It amazes me how certain moments in our lives can define us. How they can stick with us as we age, and the meanings change as we change. It's about recognizing that things need to change and then deciding what the meanings of them are for ourselves.

We got off the plane and loaded onto buses to drive us the half-hour ride to Camp Lejeune. Landing in America was exciting and emotional, but it was only us who were there to experience it, once we arrived at Camp Lejeune our families and loved ones would be there waiting for us. Some Marines and Sailors would see and hold their newborn children for the first time and everyone but me would be seeing their loved ones for the first time since early May. The emotions were running high on those buses and everyone was so excited that we all kept quiet in anticipation. As the buses approached the 2nd LAR Battalion headquarters, we could see hundreds of people gathered and the closer we got the louder the cheering and clapping got.

Marines and Sailors crowded around the bus windows to try and see their loved ones as we approached. Captain Connor momentarily snapped us out of the moment to remind us that once we met with our families, we still needed to go to the armory to drop off our rifles before we could secure for the night and leave with our loved ones. I could tell he was just as excited as the rest of us but wanted to emphasize that point before the chaos and excitement that awaited us all began when we got off the buses. We got off the buses and were rushed by the crowd of people frantic to find their Marines and Sailors that they'd waited for seven long months to see. It was a moment of pure beauty and happiness that made me realize the deployment was finally over. I made my way through the crowd and found my mom. We hugged for what seemed like an eternity and I could feel her release the burden she'd been carrying for all those months. For her, the deployment was finally over and her son was home and safe on American soil.

We quickly went to the armory to turn in our weapons, then returned to the battalion headquarters area where we had a brief company formation with our loved ones gathered around. Lt. Col. Grattan addressed us and acknowledged the sacrifices our families had made during the seven-month deployment. I'm sure he could sense that everyone wanted to get out of there and spend time with their families so he quickly released us for the night. My mom and I left Camp Lejeune and headed to the condo she had rented in Topsail Island. I had to go back and forth to Camp Lejeune during the time she stayed with me but the days were short and not much was expected of us after returning from the deployment. It was nice to be off of the base but also somewhat overwhelming to be alone with my mom after everything we had both been through. It just felt like there was so much left unsaid between us, like there was an elephant in the room that I was afraid to acknowledge. I went right back to my usual method of dealing with my emotions at the time, drinking heavily. It wasn't so much that I didn't want to be around my mom. I was just afraid to open the floodgate of emotions that was waiting to come out of me. I still greatly enjoyed the time with her and will be forever grateful for the effort she made to attend my homecoming.

When you return from a deployment, the Marine Corps keeps you on base for a few weeks before allowing you to take up to 30 days of post-deployment leave. The idea is to be able to keep an eye on Marines and Sailors and make sure they have time to decompress before being let loose into the civilian world. In theory, it is definitely a good idea but in reality, all the Marines and Sailors do is drink at the barracks or at the one bar on base called Heroes. We'd all gather at Heroes every chance we got and get drunk to the point that we'd finally start talking about what we went through on our deployments. We'd then make it back to our barracks rooms and set an alarm to stumble out and into an accountability formation in the morning to make sure we were all still alive. The days were filled with mostly administrative tasks associated with transitioning back to garrison life; they were easy days but we were all anxious to go on our post-deployment leave. By that time I was considered a "short timer" because I was getting out in June of 2010, so I began to get the usual sourness that Marines getting ready to leave active duty get. I wanted to avoid all Marine Corps garrison activities and be left alone to hang out in my room all day or go to the gym. I did what I needed to do in order to get by and not draw any negative attention to myself, but I also didn't go out of my way to help with much. I had established a great relationship with my command during the deployment so I was left alone and trusted to accomplish whatever I needed to get done.

At some point between my return from Afghanistan and post-deployment leave, I was able to meet up with Q. The 2nd Battalion 8th Marines was right down the road from 2nd LAR so it wasn't hard to find each other. There had been so much that had happened since we had last seen each other that it was difficult to know where to begin, so we started at the most obvious place, Nick's death. It was hard for me to talk to him about the funeral because I felt so guilty for not only going but also for him not being able to go. We got drunk and reminisced about our friend and made plans to keep hanging out, but as time went on, it became obvious that Nick was the common ground that held us together. We were friends, but I had met Q through Nick and all my experiences with Q were with Nick. It was hard to talk about Nick without getting emotional, so we just drank until we could deal with those emotions and finally let them out. It was a difficult time for us both. Q had his own experiences during his deployment that I'll never understand but we both had the shared sadness for our friend who died far too soon.

Post-deployment leave finally came and I went home for 30 days. I drank and partied like I was in college the entire time and had a lot of fun. I kept myself so busy that I didn't give myself a chance to think about anything too heavy or contemplate what I planned to do after my discharge from the Marines. I was a very lost person. I knew that my identity was strongly tied to being a Marine and that was coming to an end. When I gave myself enough time to think about it I began to panic. I definitely didn't want to be in the Marine Corps anymore, but I also felt like I didn't want to get out. I had always planned to get out and go to college with Nick and live the life we felt we missed out on during the four years we were enlisted. Without that plan I felt afraid about what may happen with me after getting discharged. By the time my post-deployment leave came to an end, I was ready to be back at Camp Lejeune and regain some structure in my life.

After post-deployment leave, I settled right back into my role as a short-timer in the battalion. I spent my days going to appointments on base to start narrowing down the long checklist of things that needed to be done before being discharged and going to the gym at night. It was amazing to me how quickly things got right back to the standard nonsense that is garrison life in the Marine Corps infantry. It felt like the deployment never even happened, or it was something we were supposed to just forget about. I understand that the show must go on and order and discipline is what the Marine Corps is based around, but after being deployed, all the trivial aspects of the Marine Corps bothered me even more. Uniform inspections, barracks room inspections, field trainings, cleaning weapons at the armory, and anything else to keep us busy were just old to me and served no purpose because I was getting discharged in the near future. I knew that I was at the end and my heart just wasn't in it any longer. In the Marine Corps, a deployment ends and the battalion quickly picks up where it left off and begins reorganizing the companies and platoons in order to prepare for the next deployment and training evolutions. That meant there were many new Marines who joined the unit while we were deployed and needed to be spread out amongst the battalion. It creates an atmosphere where there are new and eager Marines mixed in with many Marines like me who were just waiting to get out or wanted a break from training. Despite all of this my command continued to support me and take great care of me. I felt that there was a bond that everyone in Charlie Company had developed that transcended the much larger Marine Corps.

On May 19th, 2010, I went on what is called terminal leave. I had 30 days of leave saved up so I was allowed to use it until it ran into my discharge date of June 19th. I drove my car out of the front gate of Camp Lejeune for the last time and made the 14-hour drive home to Cape Cod, Massachusetts to start a life that I was in no way prepared for. I had made that long drive home many times before but it was a strange feeling to know that I wouldn't be coming back potentially ever again. I thought about how the whole journey had started nearly six years ago when Nick and I had joined the delayed entry program together as high school kids. Those days felt like a lifetime ago and I felt like a completely different person. It was a bittersweet day for me, knowing that I was leaving that life behind me and in a way, leaving the dream that Nick and I embarked on together behind me as well. The excitement of being free from the constraints of the Marine Corps filled me with hope that I would figure it all out. I was so grateful to be alive that I didn't care at the time what was next, but I knew that the summer of 2009 would be what shaped everything in my life going forward.

LIFE AFTER THE MARINES

I did nothing remarkable or extraordinary during my time in the Marine Corps or on either of my deployments. I joined the Marine Corps as a lost and confused kid out of high school and left it four years later as a lost and confused young man being sent back into the civilian world. Once I got out and the excitement of my freedom started to wear off, I fell into a very deep and dark hole. I felt like I was useless, like I was destined to be someone forever talking about and defined by their short time in the military. I was angry at the world, sad that my friend Nick was gone, and angry at myself for not having the strength to deal with these things and move forward. I was also drinking heavily and often in my bedroom in the basement of my mom's house where I was living. It took a turn from being a fun celebration with friends to me drinking alone just to ease the anxiety and fear of my life. As the summer of 2010 turned into fall, I made the decision to attend community college to give myself some purpose and direction. I quickly realized that it wasn't going to fulfill me and I felt so out of place that it was uncomfortable. I felt lost, scared, and alone despite the fact that I was surrounded by people willing to help me in any way they could. I fought all my internal battles alone and took it as a point of pride that no one ever had to worry about me or think that I was having a difficult time. I put on a big show that I'm sure everyone around me saw right through.

I was consumed with these feelings every day and saw no end in sight. I even considered going back into the military at one point just to escape the reality of having to figure out life on my own. I got a lot of attention for Nick's death and it ate away at me. It made me feel so ashamed and guilty for trying to take any sort of help from anyone for the benefit of my friend's life. I continued to battle with the thought that it should have been me who was killed instead of Nick, that Nick would have had his life figured out by now. These thoughts were irrational but at the time, I was too consumed by them to think logically. I was still trying to move forward but I just didn't know how, and because I didn't know how, I beat myself up even more for it. I viewed it as a weakness that needed to be eliminated from me. This went on for months until one day I came home from the gym and saw a red folder with the Marine Corps Eagle Globe and Anchor on the front of it stuck in the front door of my mom's house. I opened the folder and saw a note that said,

Dear Cpl. Coville… I mean Mr. Coville!

I just wanted to take a moment to congratulate you on this award. This is most deserving, and in all reality should be more. The impact you have made on the lives of all the Marines that you interacted with is unquantifiable. You have changed their lives for the better, and for that, they will always remember you.

To some people this award could be some metal with a colorful ribbon attached. But this is not so…it is the representation of hard work, dedication, and extreme courage that you displayed during our 7 months in Afghanistan. Please display this award proudly, and let your children and grandchildren know that their father/grandfather was a hero for the great nation of the United States of America and for its people.

I wish you well in years to come, and I am very proud to have known you and to have served with you. If there is anything that I can ever do for you, please just ask.

Take care young man and I look forward to hearing good things from you in the future.

Semper Fidelis!

Christopher S. Connor
Captain, Charlie Company 2nd LAR

Underneath that letter was a certificate awarding me a Navy and Marine Corps Achievement Medal with combat valor distinction. My platoon commander, Lt. Mahoney, had put me in for the award for the ambush and firefight that my crew and I had gotten into on July 6th and my actions during it. These awards are usually presented in a battalion formation ceremony, but because I had been discharged prior to its approval, it was sent to my new home address. This had come as a complete surprise to me. I knew that Lt. Mahoney was in the process of writing up awards for Marines but I did not know that I was one of them. I do not feel that I did anything to deserve any kind of award but I am appreciative of it nonetheless. What made the receiving of this award so special to me was the personal letter that Captain Connor had written to go along with it. The fact that the man had taken the time to write that letter meant everything to me. The award itself meant a great deal to me, but the letter Captain Connor wrote to accompany it reminded me of who I was, what I had been through, and what I was capable of. It reminded me of the identity I was quickly losing in my lost and confused state. The letter and award came at a time when I desperately needed to be reminded of what I had done a year earlier and how fortunate I was to be alive. It completely changed my mindset and lit a fire in me to move forward in life and stop living in a state of despair that was only due to my own limited thinking at the time.

As time went on I started letting my guard down and received help from many people in my life, but no one helped me more than Nick's dad, Steven Xiarhos. He put the thought in my head to become a police officer and pushed me to go to the police academy. After a year went by, I had a long enough break and knew I needed a new challenge and some serious structure in my life. I told Steve that I was ready to go to the police academy and he did everything he could to get me in the soonest one. I became extremely close with Nick's younger brother, Alex, after I had gotten out of the Marines and he decided that he would go with me. In many ways, I felt that going off to the police academy with Nick's brother was an extension of the story Nick and I had started together many years earlier. Nick was a big reason why I had the confidence to join the Marine Corps and I felt that I could help his brother in the ways Nick helped me by going through it with him. Alex and I went to the six-month-long police academy in November of 2011 and I started a whole new chapter of my life that is still unfolding today.

I played a tiny and insignificant role in the bigger picture of what occurred in that summer of 2009. My story is only one of thousands of stories that are waiting to be told by a generation of youth who volunteered to go fight for the people they love and the ideals America stands for. As time went on, the war in Afghanistan became a convoluted mess with no strategic victory or favorable end in sight, but the youth continued to go with no questions asked. To be able to serve in a combat zone for this country as a United States Marine is the greatest privilege I've ever had. It deeply saddens me that America seems to have lost its way with its divisive politics and questionable policies that seem to change far too often to fit the needs of whichever party is in power. Do I trust the institution of the United States government at this point in my life? Sadly I do not, but what I do trust is the fighting spirit of America and what it stands for. I trust that when a threat to our freedom arises the youth will always be there to answer the call. I trust that there will always be a generation of young people willing to fight and die for what they believe in to protect the ones they love. That is why we must always ensure beyond all doubt that the causes that we are willing to sacrifice American lives for are just and that there is no other alternative. Violence is an unfortunate reality of human nature and it has been proven since the beginning of humanity that there will always be wars, but that doesn't change the fact that every single life lost during war means something and that the cost of those lives is far greater than many people will ever fully realize.

AFTERWARD

Writing this story was a difficult thing to do for many reasons. As I started writing, I realized that the more I remembered the more I remembered. In the process of writing, I felt myself consumed by the mindset of being in that period of life. I relived many things I had either forgotten about or intentionally moved on from. The whole process felt therapeutic and freeing. I came to realize that once the story was written in physical form, it would allow me to not move on from it but accept it as only one part of my life and make peace with it. The events of that summer had defined my internal being for so long that it almost became a burden that prevented me from reaching my full potential in life. That's not to say that I ever want to forget those events, but I needed to make peace with them and decide what context they held in my overall life. I also had so much self-doubt in the writing process. I feared I was making a story only about me that affected so many other people, that I was glorifying my time in the Marines and that I would come across as boasting or self-centered. When I read through my journal from 15 years ago, I realized that the overarching theme and feeling of the entries was vulnerability. I knew that I wanted to tell the story through only my perspective and experiences so that I didn't disrespect or misrepresent anyone else's and center it around that journal to show that I was nothing more than a 21-year-old kid trying to figure it all out as it happened.

I hope that by reading this story, anyone who has their own story that they've been holding onto and letting define their lives finds the ability to make peace with it. Writing it down for me made it a real thing that could be put out in the world and free myself from the internal struggles associated with it. It is okay to be vulnerable, to ask for help and to talk through things. The idea of moving on from something makes me feel like you are forgetting about it and leaving it behind, but I have no desire to forget about any of this and never will. Instead, I want to move forward with it in life but with a meaning that I can be at peace with. We all have our own battles that we've fought in life and most often don't ever talk about them. There is an entire generation of veterans living amongst the civilian population that participated in the wars in Iraq and Afghanistan and every single one of them has a story of their own. I hope that as time goes on, that generation continues to find its voice and let people know what they did as they willingly participated in history and did what their country asked of them without question. I hope that anyone who has a story to tell that's come to define their lives, veteran or not, finds a way to tell it and make peace with it. If it is a big deal to you, then it is a big deal and that's all that matters.

It's been said that we all die twice, when we leave this earth and when the last person to know us speaks our names. Keep your friends and loved one's alive by sharing their stories and how much they meant to you.

ABOUT AUTHOR

Andrew Coville is a native of Massachusetts, raised on Cape Cod. He served in the Marine Corps with the 2nd Light Armored Reconnaissance Battalion from 2006 to 2010. Following his enlistment in the Marine Corps, he transitioned into law enforcement and has been serving in that capacity since 2012. A proud graduate of Curry College, this marks his debut publication.

The war in Afghanistan endured for 20 years, witnessing the repeated deployment of an all-volunteer military generation. This narrative unfolds the experiences of one young Marine who played a small role in that prolonged conflict. It delves into his firsthand account on the ground level, navigating emotions of excitement, fear, loss, and confusion at the age of 21. This work, while not a traditional memoir, serves as a snapshot into the summer of 2009, illustrating how specific life events can profoundly shape one's trajectory. It further examines the evolution of the context surrounding these events as perspectives on life shift.

Made in the USA
Middletown, DE
05 February 2024

48576109R00076